"I guess Sophia's supposed to be Madison two-point-oh these days, but I gotta say, it's not exactly working out. I miss filming with you. It's not nearly as much fun since you left," Kate said.

Music to Madison's ears! "Okay, confidentially? I do plan on coming back. I'm waiting for Trevor to meet my terms."

Kate's eyes widened. "Really? Oh my God, that is the best news ever." She seemed like she might be on the verge of rushing over and giving Madison a hug.

Madison held up a hand. She liked Kate, she honestly did, but she was never going to be the huggy type. "Yes," Madison said, smiling contentedly. "I think things are about to take a turn for the better."

Despite her words, though, Madison did worry a little that Trevor might hold a grudge because she'd ignored him for so long. But so be it. Could Trevor really blame her? He of all people should know that all was fair in love, war, and reality TV.

BOOKS BY LAUREN CONRAD

L.A. Candy

Sweet Little Lies
AN L.A. CANDY NOVEL

Sugar and Spice
AN L.A. CANDY NOVEL

The Fame Game

Starstruck
A FAME GAME NOVEL

Infamous
A FAME GAME NOVEL

LAUREN CONRAD
Style

LAUREN CONRAD
Beauty

LAUREN CONRAD

Infamous

HARPER

An Imprint of HarperCollinsPublishers

Infamous
Copyright © 2013 by Lauren Conrad

ISBN 978-0-06-207983-1 (pbk.)

Typography by Andrea Vandergrift
14 15 16 17 18   CG/RRDH   10 9 8 7 6 5 4 3 2 1
❖
First paperback edition, 2014

To Max Stubblefield.
Little of what I have today would be possible
without your guidance and friendship.
Thank you for always sticking by me . . .
and for being "singing guy."

Results for **#TheFameGame**

Tweets Top / All

@Becca B   1 min

I thought I was over @MissMadParker but I MISS her. This show sux without her. **#thefamegame**

@Suzie Klein   1 min

What is up w/Sophia? Girl is craycray. **#thefamegame**

@Becca B   1 min

LOL, where's Madison's Makeovers when you need it? **#thefamegame**

@Emma1996   2 min

What is Carmen wearing?? Gawd! **#thefamegame** #fashionpolice

---

@Emma1996   2 min

Someone plz tell Kate 2 be less boring. Girl's glued 2 couch & that Drew guy. **#thefamegame**

@Suzie Klein   2 min

BRING BACK @MISSMADPARKER #orelse **#thefamegame**

@Becca B   2 min

I wonder what's on the CW. **#thefamegame** #wherestheremote??

1

A TURN FOR THE BETTER

Madison Parker poured two large glasses of iced tea and walked, slightly slower than usual, to the table in her sunny kitchen nook. "I have sugar," she said, placing the glasses on two shell-pink linen cocktail napkins, "if you want any sweetener."

Kate Hayes raised her eyebrows in surprise, and Madison noted that her friend must have *finally* started taking some of her beauty advice. Kate's brows were perfectly tinted and shaped, as if she'd just stepped out of Anastasia Beverly Hills. *Good-bye, strawberry-blond caterpillars*, Madison thought. *You won't be missed.*

"You have actual sugar?" Kate asked. "I thought you were a Splenda-only kind of girl?"

Madison sat down across from her. Carefully. The recovery from her most recent cosmetic procedure had taken a little longer than she'd hoped. She *looked* fantastic, but she still felt a bit sore. "I think it was left here from the previous tenant," she allowed. "Along with that hideous mirror in the bathroom."

Kate glanced around at the small apartment, as if she hadn't been here a dozen times checking in on post-op Madison. Kate was the only person Madison had been willing to see, so she was Madison's source for take-out sushi, issues of the weekly mags, and information on shoots for the new season of *The Fame Game*. Like how bad it was going. How flat the scenes were, how empty the fake-impromptu dinner parties. And Madison *loved* hearing it.

"Was that spider plant left over, too?" Kate asked, nodding her head in its direction.

"No," Madison admitted. "That's mine."

She followed Kate's gaze. The spider plant was dying, and—there was no getting around it—the apartment was pretty depressing. The kitchen was the nicest room in the whole place, which was ironic for a person who rarely ate and who definitely never cooked.

She'd moved into it the day after her sudden exit from *The Fame Game*, because it was cheap (for L.A., anyway) and available.

This lack of foresight, real-estate-wise, was only one of the things Madison had come to regret. The days immediately after her on-camera explosion at the hospital were dark ones. She hadn't fully understood what PopTV meant for her, either personally or professionally. So, for the first time in her life, she was utterly alone, with absolutely *nothing* on her iCal.

Nothing but the remainder of her community-service hours, that is. Since she couldn't face Ryan Tucker (her ex? her former friend-with-benefits?), Madison claimed a sudden onset of life-threatening pet-dander allergies and requested a transfer from Lost Paws.

Connie Berkley, the straight-talking paper-pusher from the L.A. County court system, granted it grudgingly, and Madison spent the next two weeks picking up beer cans, cigarette butts, and fast-food wrappers in a Los Feliz park. She had to wear bad sneakers and a hideous Day-Glo orange vest, and the three other people working with her were beyond offensive. But at least none of them were named Ryan. At least none of them had taken her heart and stomped on it.

Every day she came home, sweaty and hot, to an apartment filled with pretty but generic furniture she'd gotten free from Crate & Barrel (she promised them she'd do an "at-home" shoot for one of the weeklies). There was no Gaby to greet her, and there were no cameras to film her. If it weren't for Kate, and for her dog, Samson, Madison would have been seriously depressed.

When she felt especially sorry for herself, Madison did her best to remember how things could always be worse. For instance: She hadn't OD'd by mistake, the way Gaby had, and she wasn't now in a locked-down rehab facility. (No at-home shoots there!) Gaby had been in treatment at the Hope Medical Center in Malibu for almost six weeks now. No doubt she was going to countless individual and group therapy sessions and getting really good at Ping-Pong.

Or was it mental hospitals where they played Ping-Pong? Madison would have to ask her, if it didn't sound too rude.

They'd been in touch a few times since Gaby's OD, but the Hope staff had confiscated Gaby's cell phone and limited her computer time, so their interactions had been brief. Also, the moment Madison finished up her community service, she'd hopped on a plane to Mexico to regroup. It was her own personal emotional rehab.

She didn't tell anyone she was going (except for Kate, who had agreed to dog-sit Samson); she simply vanished. And it felt great.

In a small town an hour outside of Cabo, Madison took long walks on the beach, ignored Trevor's five thousand phone calls, and came to a major decision. She was not done with reality TV, but she was definitely done with trying to play nice. She'd been burned by Charlie, Ryan, and Sophie (twice). It was about time she remembered that a girl couldn't trust anyone but herself.

"Madison," Trevor's voice mails always said, "we *really* have to talk."

She took great pleasure in deleting each one. She'd talk to him when she was good and ready.

But all too soon, it was time for her to return to L.A. While Madison could plot her comeback beneath a *palapa* on a Mexican beach, she could hardly *accomplish* it from there.

When she arrived back at LAX, Madison's very first phone call had been to her go-to plastic surgeon. It was time for some laser lipo, because those carbs she'd eaten when she was "happy" with Ryan were still hanging around her midsection. Dr. Klein, who had a keen nose for business (and had coincidentally done Madison's nose), had given her a deal in exchange for her participation in his "I'll never tell" press release. ("I look great after a visit with Dr. Klein. Where did he operate on me? I'll never tell!")

She smiled, thinking about it. She could probably work a similar deal with Dr. Burton the next time she needed a Botox touch-up. (She was definitely looking forward to the day when she was done paying off Luxe for the necklace Charlie stole; it was humiliating to barter for cosmetic procedures.)

"Earth to Madison," Kate said, waving a hand in front of her face.

Madison turned to her. "What? Were you saying something?"

"I've only been asking you the same question for, like, five minutes," Kate said, looking slightly insulted.

"Ask me again. Sorry, I'm listening."

Kate took a sip of her tea and then got up to find the sugar. "Are you going to go see Gaby when they let her out? We're all going to be there, you know. And that means the PopTV crew will be there, too."

"May I remind you that I quit the show?" Madison asked.

Kate rolled her eyes. "No need. I was there," she said. "But the day she gets out will be a big deal. And anyway, don't you miss being on camera? Airtime is kind of like . . . well, *air* to you."

Madison hadn't filmed anything for six weeks now—of course she missed it. Whoever said diamonds were a girl's best friend hadn't stopped to consider a camera. "Not really," she said dismissively.

Then Kate, who was still looking for the sugar, noticed the *Gossip* magazine that Madison just *happened* to leave out on the counter. "Hey, is that the issue you're in?"

Madison nodded, unable to keep a small, satisfied smile from her face. The moment her bruises had vanished, she'd set up a photo op on the beach in Malibu and paired it with an exclusive sit-down with a reporter from *Gossip*. She'd talked about her "rewarding" community service, and how it made her rethink her priorities. She had skillfully dodged the reporter's questions about trouble on the set of *The Fame Game*. Since Trevor hadn't included her "I quit" outburst on the season finale, no one really knew what was going on with her. With only a couple episodes of season two having aired, the rumors were swirling, and Madison liked it that way. The less she said, the more people wanted to know.

The best part of the article was the end, in which the writer suggested that if Madison Parker were to leave the show, *The Fame Game* would be a total snoozefest.

"Community service made you 'reexamine your celebrity lifestyle,' huh?" Kate asked, looking up from the magazine. "You learned how 'vitally important' it is to give back?" She laughed. "You're amazing, Mad, you really are."

"I try," Madison said. "Do you like how I dropped in the *verrry* subtle Carmen Curtis reference?"

Kate's eyes scanned down the page. "'"More young celebrities should perform community service," Madison says, as she sips her green tea,'" Kate read aloud. "'"No one should be above the law, whether they steal a car, a diamond necklace, or a designer top."'" Kate looked up, her eyes wide. "Madison. That's not exactly subtle."

Madison shrugged. "Carmen doesn't read those things anyway, and I doubt you're going to tell her about it, even if she is your new roomie."

"True . . . ," Kate said. Trevor had made her and Carmen move into Madison and Gaby's apartment; it was all set up for filming, and otherwise it would be sitting vacant. Madison knew that Kate wasn't entirely happy with this arrangement. She wasn't sure why Kate and Carmen had such a hard time getting along (though maybe it had something to do with their habit of picking the same guy to be involved with, whether he was a handsome Aussie actor or a tattooed musical intern . . .).

Samson trotted into the room and flopped down at Madison's feet. She leaned over and gave his head a rub. "You're my community service, aren't you, boy? If it weren't for my selfless heart, I'd have ordered myself a cute teacup Chihuahua like Paris Hilton's."

Kate choked on her tea.

Madison shot her a look. "What?"

"Sorry," Kate said, wiping her mouth and smiling. "'Selfless' is maybe not the *first* word I'd use to describe you."

"Of course not," Madison said. "That would be 'fabulous,' right?"

"Oh, totally," Kate agreed. "So, fabulous Madison, are you going to show up for Gaby's release or what? Because I, personally, would really love to see you there and I'm sure Gaby would too. I guess Sophia's supposed to be Madison two-point-oh these days, but I gotta say, it's not exactly working out. I miss filming with you. It's not nearly as much fun since you left."

Music to Madison's ears! "I want to be there for Gaby, but I'm not sure about the timing. . . ." She paused, relishing the moment. "Okay, confidentially? I do plan on coming back. I'm waiting for Trevor to meet my terms."

Kate's eyes widened. "Really? Oh my God, that is the best news ever." She seemed like she might be on the verge of rushing over and giving Madison a hug.

Madison held up a hand. She liked Kate, she honestly did, but she was just never going to be the huggy type.

Also, she was still sore. She got up and dumped the remains of her tea into her spider plant. (Extra nutrients, right?)

"Yes," Madison said, smiling contentedly. "I think things are about to take a turn for the better."

Despite her words, though, Madison did worry a little that Trevor might hold a grudge because she'd ignored him for so long. But so be it. Could Trevor really blame her? He of all people should know that all was fair in love, war, and reality TV.

2

THE RULES OF UNOFFICIAL
COHABITATION

Carmen tried the bathroom door—*locked*—and then knocked loudly on it. Yes, there was another bathroom in the apartment she shared with Kate, but that one didn't have the tube of her favorite lipstick sitting on the counter.

"Hang on a minute," called a voice. A male voice.

Carmen sighed. Drew. Again.

A month ago she'd been complaining that she hardly ever saw her childhood best friend, and now it seemed like he was everywhere she turned. At the breakfast table, eating her cereal. On the living room couch, watching a Lakers game. In the bathroom, holding her cosmetics hostage. Like Carmen's dad sometimes said: Be careful what you wish for.

She flounced back into the dining room where the cameras had been set up. Kate was sitting at the table, eating a bowl of Froot Loops. She went through two or three boxes of it a week; she had the appetite of a twelve-year-old boy. Lucky for her, she seemed to have the metabolism of one, too.

"Cameras roll as soon as I finish this," Kate said. Trevor's aversion to filming them eating was well known. "I was *starving*."

"No rush. I was kind of hoping to get my lipstick. . . ."

"You look beautiful, as always," Laurel called.

Carmen laughed as she sat down at her designated seat at the table. "Like I can trust *you*," she said. "You just want to get started."

Laurel shrugged. "What can I say? Time is money."

In another few moments, Kate was done, and Bret the camera guy had taken his usual place behind his Sony Hi Def, but Drew had still not emerged. Carmen was annoyed she hadn't been able to get to her lipstick. Now she'd look washed out, which was fine when they were filming early-morning scenes, but less fine when it was 11 a.m. and she was otherwise ready to face the world. Her floral silk button-down practically *demanded* a coat of NARS's Funny Face.

Kate brushed a Froot Loop crumb from her shirt and offered Carmen a small smile.

Carmen smiled back, though she was still annoyed, and then took a sip of her tea. (Drinking on camera was totally fine, of course.) "So, do you think Gaby'll be different?" she asked Kate, exactly as she was supposed to.

"I think she'll be in a better place," Kate said.

Carmen laughed. "'A better place'? I thought that was

what you said when someone died."

Kate looked mildly affronted. "You know what I mean. Like, emotionally."

"Sorry," Carmen said. "I was kidding." Then she bit her lip and gazed down into her mug.

She'd been excited to move in with Kate for a couple of reasons—(a) she had no other place to live at the moment; and (b) she thought they might finally fully make up—but so far it'd been harder than she'd hoped. They kept offending each other in the little ways. Carmen, for example, had invited a few friends over without telling Kate. Then Kate had eaten all of Carmen's leftover lo mein. Carmen had shrunk one of Kate's two decent sweaters in the dryer, and then Kate had made some snide comment about Hollywood royalty not knowing how the real world worked. . . .

They still *liked* each other, they really did. But for some reason they were having a hard time showing it.

Carmen wondered if things would ever go back to the way they had been before Luke Kelly walked into their lives. Of course, Carmen was really glad that he *had*, but he definitely complicated things. Pre-Luke, Kate and Carmen had been great friends, and Carmen was realizing more and more how hard those were to come by.

She looked up again. Time to get on the ball and give the camera *something*. "Gaby sent me a letter a couple of weeks ago," Carmen said. "She said she was learning how to let go of unhealthy influences and finding her inner strength. She said her mantra was 'Healthy Choices.'" Then she giggled; she couldn't help it. "I think that's a brand of soup."

"Well, if it works for her, I'm all for it," Kate said. "But I bet she's embarrassed at all this. I mean, wouldn't you be?"

Carmen shrugged. "I don't know. It's not like she's the first person to get confused about the right dosage of her medication."

She shot Kate a look. Surely Kate hadn't forgotten that she'd taken too much Xanax and turned into a walking zombie on national television. (Trevor would cut that line, no doubt, but Carmen hadn't been able to resist.)

Kate only blinked at her, as if she really *had* forgotten.

"I'm actually really happy for her," Carmen went on. "I think being at Hope was just what she needed. A break. Time to clear her head."

Carmen wished she could have a break, too. Not at rehab, obviously, but say . . . a week at Miravel Resort & Spa? Having a few weeks off from filming had been great, but it wasn't as if she'd been able to take a break from the *rest* of her life. From the tabloids, which continued to print lies about her, as well as some private truths. From Sophia, who had taken to calling her daily to talk about how cute their new producer was. And from Krew (or Date—they both worked), who were usually stuck together like Siamese twins.

Speak of the devil (or one half of it), Drew emerged from the bathroom. In a short pink towel.

Granted, he was out of the shot, but still—hadn't he learned to take *clothes* into the bathroom? Wasn't that one of the first rules of unofficial cohabitation?

He gave Carmen a small, apologetic wave. Kate hadn't seen him, thankfully, so she was still focused on the scene. "I wonder if Madison will be there with us," Kate said.

"Yeah. I wonder if Trevor's going to be able to woo her back."

Carmen knew that line wouldn't make it to air, either, but it didn't matter. Laurel had already informed them that they were going to shoot this segment several times. "So we have the right lead-in," she'd explained. Since Gaby was getting out in two days and no one knew whether Madison would show up or not, they needed to cover their bases.

According to the reality of *The Fame Game*, Madison had taken a long vacation after finishing her community service. Some kind of *Eat, Pray, Love* thing, where she was finding herself and rededicating her life to . . . something or other. This explanation was buying Trevor time until he could get her back on the show. *If* he could.

For the first take, Kate and Carmen talked a bit about Madison's vacation, and how she was still "in Mexico." (This was awkward, because Madison had already been photographed at the airport last week returning from Mexico, and Gaby's release date would be written about—so the timing wouldn't work. But Carmen had her directions, so she followed them.) Next they shot a conversation in which they suggested that Madison, while back in L.A., was still too upset by Gaby's overdose to face her. Finally, there was the cliff-hanger scene: Madison had told Kate she'd be there and had told Carmen that she wouldn't. *Which would it be? The world holds its breath!*

That was the winner, Carmen thought, no question. Trevor could never resist a cliffhanger.

Drew passed by again, this time fully clothed and in view of the cameras. And Kate. Her eyes followed him into the kitchen, and there was a love-struck look on her face. "I wish Madison—*and* Gaby—could find a good guy," she said.

Carmen put her head in her hands. Was it possible to die of annoyance? Because she felt like she might.

Then she looked up. "We could lend them Drew," she said, smiling.

"We?" Kate asked.

Carmen shrugged. "You know what I mean."

"Do I?" Kate asked, a slight edge coming into her voice.

God, what was her problem? Carmen stood up. "Well, anyway," she said, pointing to her watch. "I've gotta go meet with my agent."

"Yeah, that's a wrap on this scene," Laurel called,

stepping out from behind Bret. "You are both free until the day after tomorrow, when we welcome Ms. Garcia back into reality."

Carmen hurried into the bathroom to fetch her lipstick, thinking how those words were probably the *last* ones that would apply to whatever was going to happen to Gaby.

3

DON'T MAKE ME CALL THEM MYSELF

Trevor sucked grimly on an ice cube as he sat in the editing bay at PopTV Studios. Before him were half a dozen computer screens, and each displayed raw footage from the past few weeks of season-two shooting. *Kate and Carmen shopping. Sophia trying to bend Kate into pigeon pose. Carmen on a phone call with her publicist. Kate and Drew curled up on her couch, recapping her most recent performance.* Each clip made him want to—well, depending on his mood, either fall asleep . . . or jump out a window.

He spun around in his swivel chair, and Laurel eyed him nervously. He'd already thrown one fit today, and she was probably bracing herself for round two. He'd promoted her to executive producer, but the old listen-to-Trevor-when-he-freaks-out part of her job description remained.

"That Kate and Drew scene could be intercut with shots of Carmen looking wistful," she suggested.

"Oh really?" he said facetiously. "I *never* would have thought of that."

Trevor crunched the ice cube from his latte and fished another one from his cup. With Gaby in rehab and Madison AWOL, he was trying to make a show with half his regular cast. He'd managed to patch together the final few episodes of season one, using old footage of the main girls and some new footage featuring Sophia more prominently. What a nightmare that had been. He'd used an army of interns to comb through unused scenes, and there were too many continuity problems to count. Gaby had had a Restylane mishap (for a couple of days it looked as if she'd been punched in the mouth), Madison had put on a few pounds during the Ryan weeks (though it looked great on her), and Kate had taken a weekend trip to Palm Springs, but she might as well have taken a nap in a tanning bed (she came back looking more like a *Jersey Shore* reject than an up-and-coming musician).

Then the ratings came in, which showed a troubling dip; in particular, audiences did not respond well to Sophia's bigger role. They liked her in the background well enough, but the moment she stepped into the spotlight, people starting changing the channel.

At least Gaby's OD, while unfortunate for all sorts of reasons, had played out well on screen. He'd found footage of Madison and Gaby at a café, in which Madison looked worried about her friend, so he'd used that. He'd even been able to fall back on the footage of her storming out of the massage room that day, cleverly editing it so it looked like Gaby's drug problem was what had made Madison so upset.

Yes, he had managed to create an excellent season finale, if he did say so himself. The shots of the girls in the waiting room, their eyes brimming with tears—well, that had been some seriously moving television.

There was a knock on the door, and Trevor barked out, "Who is it?"

Stephen Marsh, the newest *Fame Game* producer, poked his head in. "Hope is trying to renege on their offer to let us film on site," he said.

Trevor glared at him. "Don't let them off the hook," he said. "And *don't* make me call them myself," he added. He turned to Laurel. "Make sure he handles this right, okay?"

Laurel nodded and followed Stephen out, and Trevor returned to his thoughts.

He'd given his girls a break over the holidays, but now it was time to get things rolling again. Carmen's regular appearance in the tabloids was good for ratings (the fight with her mom was great, though it killed him that he hadn't captured it on film), and he hoped it would last. Carmen was a smart girl; she knew what made good TV. The problem was, she didn't always bother to make it. For instance, she seemed to be involved with Luke Kelly again, this time for real. Why couldn't that guy just go away?

He'd served his purpose for the show, and now he was simply a nuisance. He wasn't even in *the country*, and yet he was monopolizing Carmen's romance story line.

On the bright side, Laurel had suggested that the Kate-Drew hookup might be getting on Carmen's nerves. Trevor had moved Carmen and Kate into Madison and Gaby's old place. He'd figured he'd get good footage of the show's two rising stars living together—but he hadn't predicted Drew's near-constant presence. If Kate didn't stop hanging all over him, Carmen Curtis—the privileged girl who'd always gotten her way—was going to snap.

It would take only a tiny little push. . . .

And Kate Hayes, while certainly not the most charismatic girl he'd ever filmed, was now huge in the Midwest. (If he ever sent her back to Ohio again, he felt certain she'd be carried away by a mob of screaming tweens.) Trevor felt confident that Kate's appeal would only grow as she pursued her music career more fully in season two.

There was always good old Jay, too. For reasons that Trevor couldn't fathom, Jay had become a fan favorite. Maybe there was something about his blend of frat-guy fart jokes and pseudo-philosophical BS that really appealed to the *Fame Game* audience. So, even though Gaby said they'd broken up because of one of her steps (she couldn't remember which it was, but it had something to do with "taking personal inventory"), Trevor would make sure they had lots of run-ins over the next few months.

The only real problem was Madison Parker. The show

needed her desperately. He knew she was back in town and that she was at least open to talking—or her agent was, anyway. What Trevor didn't know was what it would take to get her back in front of the PopTV cameras. He supposed he'd find out soon enough how dearly he'd have to pay for her return.

4

THE VOICE OF AN ANGEL

"So where's our third roommate?" Carmen asked, wandering into the living room and flopping down on one of the giant floor cushions.

Kate looked up at her, trying to decide if Carmen was being jokey or snide. "He's at Rock It! I think. But I'm not sure. It's not like I know where he is every second of the day." *Just most of the seconds*, Kate added silently.

She and Drew had been dating since she got back from Ohio. It was as if everything had suddenly fallen into place. They didn't wonder if dating would ruin their friendship, or if other people in their lives would complicate things too much (Carmen and Luke, *ahem*). They saw each other on the morning after Gaby's incident, and they'd pretty much spent every day together since. It was, in a word, fantastic.

"Is his internship still going well?" Carmen asked.

"Totally," Kate said. "He's been promoted from intern to paid intern since he's returned to school. It's only

24

minimum wage, but it's something." She smiled.

Carmen nodded. "Awesome," she said, and then began picking at one of her fingernails.

Kate turned back to the fan mail that she'd been rifling through. On Drew's and Trevor's advice, she'd finally gotten herself a manager, Todd Barrows, who had forwarded on the large stacks of letters. Todd was an old pro (he'd repped $erena when she was starting out, and that girl had *five songs* on the charts). Kate was learning a lot about the music business from both him and Drew. Though their advice often contradicted each other's.

She was also learning from her own experience. Such as: Success is not lasting, and it is never guaranteed.

That was a lesson she hadn't enjoyed much. "Starstruck" was no longer on every playlist, and her follow-up song didn't become the hit she'd hoped it would. She did *not* plan on being a one-hit wonder, and she'd been working like crazy to get another song ready to record. She was up until two the night before, and planned to be up at least that late tonight. (Laurel had even told her to take it easy: "Your under-eye bags are showing on camera. You either need more sleep or a good concealer," she'd said.)

Kate picked up an unopened letter and tapped it against her palm. She knew that reading it would make her feel better; each note was a vote of confidence, and an ego boost. She still couldn't believe that she, little Kate Hayes from Columbus, Ohio, was getting *fan mail*. So far she'd managed to write everyone back (teen girls from all over the world, plus a handful of sensitive boys), but as the stacks grew taller—and they would; they already were, despite her dip in the charts—she'd have to give up that goal. She had her Twitter account and her Facebook fan page, so she could stay connected, but she was going to feel guilty once she stopped answering letters.

"So what's up with your music?" Carmen asked, having successfully removed her hangnail.

Kate sighed. "A lot—and also sort of nothing."

"What do you mean?"

"Well, as you probably know, Trevor wouldn't let me sign a record deal before, because he felt like it was a quote-unquote 'season two story line.' So he basically made me put my life and career on hold because it suited him and his show."

"Which is also our show," Carmen pointed out.

Kate waved this obvious fact away. "Of course, but back in the fall people were calling me. My song was *everywhere*, and now it's only on that stupid Nokia commercial."

"Hey! That stupid commercial paid for your Mini Cooper."

"True," Kate said, brightening. She loved that car. "Anyway, Trevor says I can sign a deal now, but all of a sudden, my phone's not ringing."

"Oh, you'll have your pick of labels," Carmen assured her. "Your songs are great."

"Thanks," Kate said. "Maybe people are still interested,

sure. But it wasn't any fun to put them off, you know? Imagine if Colum McEntire had told you he wanted you to star in his movie, and you were like, Yeah, sounds great, but can you please wait for three months, because my dad grounded me for shoplifting?"

Carmen laughed. "Ouch. You *know* I never actually stole anything, right?"

Kate looked at her in surprise. "You didn't? And here I was, thinking Trevor must have an eye for the thieving type."

"I can't believe I never told you," Carmen said. "I took the fall for a friend."

"Wow, that was really nice of you."

Carmen shrugged. "It seemed like the right idea at the time." She sounded like she might have had second thoughts. "My dad was furious at me."

"Honestly, I felt awkward ever bringing it up, but now that I know you didn't do it, you have to tell me what really happened," Kate said.

"It's not really that exciting," Carmen said. "I didn't have to go to court like Mad."

Kate laughed. "Thank goodness there was no 'giving back to the community' required of you! Because why on earth would you want to do that?"

"Yeah," Carmen said faintly.

Kate wondered if she'd managed to offend her. Again. Why was it so hard for them to get along? It was like they couldn't help pushing each other's buttons. She'd simply meant that it was good Carmen didn't have to go to court, but it had come out sounding like Kate thought she was a spoiled brat.

"Soooooo . . . ," Kate said, after an awkward moment of silence.

"So Luke called," Carmen said suddenly. "He said filming's going great."

"Oh! That's great."

Lately it seemed as if Carmen mentioned Luke about twenty times a day. Not that Kate minded—she was completely over him. Carmen and Luke could absolutely have each other . . . for the five minutes that they'd actually be into it. If there was one thing Kate had learned about these actor types, it was that they changed partners as often (at least) as they changed roles.

What she had with Drew, on the other hand, was *real*.

Kate tapped the unopened letter against her hand once more and then tore it open. She didn't mean to read it while she and Carmen were in the middle of a conversation, but she couldn't help but glance down.

—think it's so, so unfair when people say you're boring and stuff, because you're the sweetest one of—

Kate looked back up, feeling deflated. *Thanks for the backhanded compliment, Misty from Nebraska*, she thought. As if she weren't perfectly aware of the nasty things that got said

28

about her—that she was a doormat, she was as exciting as watching paint dry—some "fan" had to go and remind her.

She tossed the letter into the garbage. She'd start her policy of not writing back with Misty.

Carmen handed her another letter and then got up. "I'm heading to bed. Gotta get my beauty sleep before Gaby's big day. Otherwise *D-lish*'ll post about how beat-down I look or something, and they'll be right."

"Night," Kate called out. She gazed at the next envelope for a moment before opening it. It was sent from here in L.A., and the handwriting was small and exquisitely neat. J.B. from Studio City: The initials and the handwriting were familiar. He'd written her before, hadn't he? Yes, and she'd sent him a signed head shot. He was probably writing to thank her—after all, not every TV personality would be so generous with her time and photos. She opened the letter, feeling rather pleased with herself for being so nice, and with J.B. for being so polite.

Dear Kate,
Thank you so much for the photo. I have it framed next to my bed. I've watched you since the very first episode of The Fame Game. *You are a great talent, and you are better and more beautiful than anyone else on that show. I love your voice. It's the voice of an angel.*

Kate smiled. Now *this* was more like it. She read on.

I wish that your voice could be the first thing I heard in the morning and the last thing I heard at night. Sometimes when I see you on TV, and your blue eyes turn toward the camera, I swear that you are looking straight at me. Telling me that you see me, and you want to get to know me. Well, I want to get to know you, too. I know it sounds silly, but sometimes I tell people you are my girl-friend—and who knows? Maybe someday you will be. I mean, look how close we live to each other.

Kate looked at the second page enclosed in the enve-lope. It was a map with what she assumed was his home circled and a line leading to a second location. She looked a little closer and realized it was their apartment. Sure, a few photographers had figured out where they lived after following them home, but Trevor had always assured them that most people didn't know.

Kate looked up. "Uh . . . Carmen?" she called.

"Brushing my teeth!" she yelled from the bathroom.

"Can you come out here and look at this letter?"

A few seconds later, Carmen came and took the let-ter and the map from Kate, her eyes quickly scanning the pages. "Oh no," she said as she read. "Ewww." When she was done, she handed the letter back to Kate as if it were contaminated. "You need to tell someone about this."

"It's not some random weird thing I can, like, ignore?"

Carmen shook her head. "That guy sounds like a

30

stalker and he clearly knows where you live. Where *we* live. My mom's had about five hundred stalkers, and trust me, they're bad news. You need to get rid of him, stat."

"Really? I mean, sure, it's kind of weird," Kate said. "But it's not like he wrote 'I'm outside your window' or something."

"Kate, people can be crazy. They watch the show and see you in your bedroom talking about your life and think that they know you."

"I think you're overreacting," Kate said. "He's just some weirdo—"

"Yeah," Carmen interrupted. "He's a weirdo. And angry weirdos are *exactly* the kind of people you want to be careful around. They can be dangerous."

Kate, admittedly, had been sort of freaked out by the letter. But something about Carmen's response annoyed her. Couldn't she simply have a rabid fan? Why did he have to be some sort of *threat*?

"I don't think—"

"You don't need to think," Carmen interrupted. Again. "Turn the letter in to Laurel and she'll give it to whoever heads security at the network. If anything, they like to have these things on file."

Kate couldn't help herself then. She was annoyed and she lashed out. "Maybe you're jealous," she whispered. "Maybe you wish you'd gotten a letter like this."

Carmen stared at her in disbelief. "Girl, if you think that, you are even more out of touch than the creep who wrote you that letter." Then she turned and stomped away.

Kate looked at the letter again. It was written on scented stationery.

Love always,
J .B.

P.S. Hope to see you very soon.

She shuddered, and then pulled out her phone and texted Laurel. Immediately after that, she texted Drew. CRAZY FAN LETTERS. CARM SAYS I SHOULD WATCH OUT. CALL ME?

But Drew did better than call her. He left Rock It! right away and drove to her apartment, even though she tried to tell him that it wasn't necessary.

The moment she opened the door and saw him, clutching a spray of daisies, standing there so tall and strong and reassuring, she couldn't believe she'd tried to convince him (and herself) that he shouldn't come.

It ended up being one of the best nights ever. They streamed *Walk the Line,* the Johnny Cash biopic, on Netflix, and cuddled on the couch. As Kate rested her cheek against Drew's warm chest, feeling his arm tight around her shoulders, she thought about the irony of it all: how the very day that Carmen seemed to think she could be in some kind of danger was also the day that she felt the most taken care of. The most safe.

Kate looked up at Drew, and he looked down at her. They smiled at each other—wide, silly, happy grins. It was great.

And then they kissed, and that was even better.

5

HOW TO MAKE AN ENTRANCE

In the parking lot of Hope Medical Center, the girls were miked and directed to stand near the building's portico awaiting Gaby's arrival. The sun felt blazingly hot; L.A. was in the middle of a freak January heat wave, and Carmen hadn't dressed appropriately for it.

"I wonder if Gaby'll get some kind of diploma," Kate said. "My cousin's kid got a diploma from her daycare."

Wow. Was Kate *trying* to sound as dense as Gaby? "I got a diploma from driving school," Carmen offered.

"All I got was a key chain that said 'Stay Alive—Drive Fifty-Five.' I mean, how *old* do you think that thing was? The speed limit hasn't been fifty-five since before I was born."

Carmen laughed. "It's vintage! Maybe it's worth something."

"Doubtful. Anyway, I threw it away." Kate squinted at the rehab. "When are they releasing Gaby?" she wondered.

"They probably already did," Carmen said drily. "And

34

Laurel's making her wait on the other side of the door until Sophia arrives and we can film."

"Did I hear my name?" Sophia hurried up to them in a cloud of lavender essence and kissed them both on the cheek. "So good to see you," she said, giving Carmen's arm a squeeze. "I wish Madison could be here, too."

Yeah, I'll bet you do, thought Carmen.

"This is such an important moment," Sophia went on, beaming at them.

"Didn't you spend some time in this place?" Carmen asked, referring to Sophia's own rehab stint, which had begun not long after she'd joined the cast of *L.A. Candy*.

"No, I went to Promises," she said breezily. "I learned so much there. It was a *fantastic* experience, and I wouldn't trade it for the world."

"Any minute now, ladies," Laurel called.

Carmen smoothed a strand of hair away from her face. She'd forgotten how much of filming was standing around, waiting. Movies were a thousand times worse in this regard, but at least you got a trailer to hang out in.

A long black town car pulled into the lot, right next to the PopTV van. A moment later, the back door opened and Trevor emerged. He gave the girls a nod and a half smile.

"What is Trevor doing here? He *never* comes to shoots," Kate said.

"Only the really big ones," Carmen corrected her. She wasn't surprised to see their executive producer here. Not out of concern for Gaby, of course, but for the footage. This would be a crucial scene for the show, so it made sense that he'd want to keep a close eye on how it went.

She watched him as he walked over to Stephen Marsh, the new producer, and she was about to ask him if they could start filming before all their makeup melted off when she saw, out of the corner of her eye, a flash of red.

She looked back toward the town car and watched, in shock, as Madison Parker emerged from the backseat, in a fantastic scarlet Dolce, looking tan, thin, and triumphant. (A bit overdressed, but still—stunning.)

Sophia gasped.

Carmen watched with grudging admiration as Madison approached them. The girl sure knew how to make an entrance.

"Oh, shit," Sophia whispered.

Carmen turned to her with a smile. She, for one, was *glad* Madison was back. They might not like each other that much, but no one could argue that Madison didn't make things interesting. "Like my dad always says," Carmen whispered back, "be careful what you wish for."

6

CUE THE HOLLYWOOD HUNKS

"—And once, I ate thirty hot dogs in fifteen minutes," bragged the blond, blue-eyed guy sitting across the table from Madison at Fig & Olive. "My friends were like, 'Dude, you should take it professional.'"

Madison flagged down the waiter, who was obviously unnerved by the PopTV film crew he'd been instructed to ignore. "Vodka and soda," she said, the instant he was within earshot. "A double—and the *sooner the better.*"

Trevor hadn't wasted any time getting her back on camera, once they'd settled on terms. He'd come *crawling* to her in the end, appearing on her doorstep all smiles and promises; she'd simply handed him an envelope from her lawyer, which contained her new, extensive demands listed on four pages of creamy white paper.

Trevor may have put his foot down at Madison's request for white peonies at every location (hey, it had worked for J.Lo), but she'd put that in there precisely so he would have something to refuse. It was business negotiations with a dash of psychological warfare. It helped that she knew from Kate how much Laurel and Trevor wanted her in the Gaby's-release scene. The look of unhappy surprise on Sophie's face when she saw her was an added bonus.

She would move in with Gaby again (in the Park Towers *penthouse*), do her best not to freeze out Sophie, and do a better job of tolerating the presence of Jay whenever Trevor sent him over. She'd also agreed to develop a romance story line. Not because she was searching for romance—she was done with *that* business (do you hear that, Ryan Tucker?)—but because she wanted screen time. There simply weren't enough dates during season one, and both she and Trevor knew it. So: Cue the Hollywood hunks.

Such as Greg, the blond, blue-eyed surfer type, currently boring her to death with a story of the "time he hooked up with Lindsay Lohan" and a bad Jon Hamm impression. Yes, she was going to need more than patience to get through this date.

This documented date.

Madison managed to smile at the drink when it appeared, and then transferred that smile to Greg's strong-jawed face. It was really too bad he couldn't keep his gorgeous mouth shut.

"So," she said, "how long have you lived in L.A.?"

"About two years now," Greg said. "I moved here from Nebraska."

"And what do you do here?" Madison already knew the answer. It was the same thing that almost everyone who moved to Hollywood from flyover country did. They acted—and by "acted," they meant they bartended by night and auditioned by day.

"I'm an actor," Greg said, putting a giant hand into the paper cone of truffle fries and pulling out a fistful.

"Really? What would I have seen you in?"

Greg paused for a moment. "A few, uh, independent shorts. I also do a little modeling on the side."

"So, right now, you aren't exactly a working actor?" She smiled slyly.

Again, Madison knew very well the answer to this question. If Greg had a paying acting job, he would not be sitting across the table feigning interest in dating someone he had nothing in common with, hoping to gain the exposure that would result in his being "discovered."

"We've all gotta start somewhere, don't we? Not everyone can get paid to be on PopTV getting frozen yogurt and shopping with her friends," Greg said through his own sly smile.

Madison sat up straighter. This date wasn't going anywhere and she knew it. Trevor would *never* air the footage if it continued like this.

"Let's order you another drink," she said, patting his hand. "And then you can tell me what it's like to attend acting classes all day while still being supported by your parents."

Greg's eyes got wide. "Excuse me?" he said, looking caught off guard.

Madison winked at him.

Behind Greg's head, she could see Julian the camera guy focusing in. She suspected he felt sorry for Greg.

"Dude," Greg said, "I don't know what your problem is, but . . ."

"I don't have a problem. I'm simply curious how you are an actor if you don't actually act."

"I'm acting right now," he said sharply. "I'm acting like I actually want to be on this date with you, even though you're a total bitch."

Madison smiled calmly. "And once again you aren't getting paid, so this must be right up your alley."

Then she stood up, grabbed her Celine bag, and exited stage left. Sure, she'd agreed to go out on dates—but she'd made no promises about *staying* out.

"Okay, let's take a look at the latest candidates for the job of Tolerable Dinner Date." Kate slid in a DVD vaguely labeled AUDITIONS 1/2013 and then hurried to join Madison on the couch.

Madison put her feet up on the coffee table and settled in. That was the good part about a bad date: A girl could get home early. "Gab, can you *please* turn down the tango music?" she called.

Trevor had promised Gaby an audition for *Dancing with the Stars*. And while watching Gaby attempt fox-trots around their new living room got tiresome, at least it had the potential to spice up her story line. Because at this point—as terrible as it was to say—the best thing Gaby had ever done for the show was overdose on painkillers.

Gaby obediently turned down the stereo and came bouncing over to the couch. "Where's the eye candy?" she asked.

Madison hit the remote. Her spirits lifted as a handsome black-haired guy walked into the frame of the screen and sat down on a stool. If she was going to play the game and go on the dates, it was only fair that her producers found her some guys who weren't utter cretins.

"Tell us your name, please." Laurel's voice came from somewhere out of frame.

"Jackson Trask," the guy said.

Madison noted his broad shoulders and his toned—but not too beefy—arms. So far, so good.

"Where are you from, and what brought you to L.A.?"

Jackson shifted in his seat and smiled right into the camera lens. Madison smiled back as if he could see her. He was a natural. "I'm from Wisconsin—go Packers!—and I've been here for a year and a half. I live in Studio City now."

"What do you do?"

"I'm developing my portfolio . . . and, uh, waiting tables at Mr. Chow's."

"Your portfolio?" Laurel asked. Madison was pretty sure she could hear her take a sip of coffee.

Jackson nodded. "Modeling. I've done a few shoots. I could have done more, but, well, sometimes the photographers ask for . . . special favors."

"Mmm," Laurel said.

"Oh my God, I've heard about that," Gaby said. "You know what he means, right? He means *sexual* favors."

"Shhh," Madison said.

Then Laurel asked Jackson if he'd dated girls in L.A., and if he considered himself a romantic, and what he was looking for in a girlfriend.

"I like to bring a girl flowers," Jackson said. "I like a girl to look good, so I don't mind shopping with her."

Then he went on to talk about how close he was with his mother, and how he loved kids, and how he was protective of his female friends—even his exes (only two!). "I mean, feminism hasn't quite caught up to our basic biology," Jackson said. "I think that women, no matter how strong they are, still want someone who can take care of them. And I want to be *that guy*."

By this point, Madison was ready to fling up her hands and flee the room. "This guy is one hundred percent lying," she said. "Like a girl with half a mind can't see through his lines? Next!"

"I thought he seemed really nice," Gaby said softly.

"No way," Kate said, shaking her head. "Mad's right. That guy was making *everything* up. He's probably not even from Wisconsin."

Gaby shrugged. "Well, I don't like nice guys that much, anyway."

She got up and did a quick little dance routine around

the living room, and Madison took the opportunity to once again appreciate her new place. Trevor's penny-pinching plan to put Kate and Carmen into Madison's old apartment had certainly backfired: By the time Gaby got released from rehab, Kate's former pad had been rented out to a pair of Las Vegas newlyweds. The only available apartment big enough for filming was the penthouse, which had four large bedrooms, three *giant* bathrooms, and a soaking tub so enormous Madison could practically swim laps.

"Ready for bachelor number two?" Kate asked, poking Madison with the *Vogue* magazine she'd been flipping through.

"I guess," Madison said.

Next they listened to an interview with a BMX biker—not because Madison would ever date him, but because he was comic relief—and then they sat through a conversation between Laurel and a Seattle native named Brian, who was in his first year of law school at UCLA. He seemed perfect until it was revealed that he didn't like dogs. Madison picked up Samson and gave him a giant kiss on the nose. "We can't have that, can we, Sammy?" she cooed.

"This is harder than I would have thought," Kate noted. "Like they say, 'Water, water everywhere, and not a drop to drink.'"

"Maybe Trevor's picking jerks on purpose," Madison mused.

"Payback for the drama?" Kate asked, smiling. "The quitting?"

"Yeah, and for the extensive, expensive rider," Madison answered. She still felt a little thrill every time she thought about her revised contract. Her (and her trusted attorney's) powers of negotiation had served her well over the years, from landing her first menial job in L.A. to securing her latest triumph, a campaign with an up-and-coming British makeup line (time to grow her brand on the other side of the pond!).

"You want to borrow Jay for a night, Mad?" Gaby asked.

Madison tried not to scoff. "Um, no thanks," she said, unable to hide her disapproval.

"My counselor said he didn't think Jay was good for me, but Trevor says he's fine. And I feel like Trevor's always looked out for me," Gaby said.

Madison couldn't precisely agree with that. When had Trevor looked out for anyone but himself? (Which, of course, was a trait Madison respected. Especially since her recent efforts to look out for *other* people had resulted in criminal charges.)

"Just admit that you still like him," Kate said, poking Gaby with a toe.

Gaby nodded. "Yeah, I totally do. What can I say? I like bad boys. Also, oh my God, you should see the new Harley he got."

Madison remembered when she felt that way about bad boys, too. Then Ryan Tucker—responsible, sane, generous Ryan Tucker—had changed everything.

Damn him.

As much as Madison wanted him out of her mind, Ryan simply wouldn't go. When she'd been with Greg earlier, she'd found herself wishing desperately that he would vanish, and that Ryan would appear in his place. Even if that meant the camera had to vanish, too.

7

GOING NOWHERE BUT UP

Carmen dipped her spoon into her frozen yogurt, carefully mixing in the bits of Heath Bar. She hadn't been to Yogurtland in months, and she wanted to savor her first bite.

"You gonna eat that or just gaze at it lovingly?" Fawn demanded. She was halfway done with her Death by Chocolate cone already.

Lily laughed. "Carmen knows how to pace herself, unlike *some* people."

"Whatever," Fawn said, taking another big lick. "It's going to melt all over her blouse."

Carmen put the spoon in her mouth and closed her eyes. Salted caramel. *Delicious.*

Kate had been home when she left and had asked what she was up to, as if she wanted to hang out, but lately Carmen felt happier and more at ease without her. So she'd lied and said that she was going straight to her parents' house. But things were never tense with Fawn and Lily like that. Once those two had gotten over their initial mis-trust of each other, they'd all hung out constantly. It was fun. Easy. Silly. Of all the amazing things that had come from scoring the lead role in *The End of Love*, getting Lily as her makeup artist was among the top. Lily had turned into a great friend.

"Whatever yourself, Fawn," Lily teased. "You look like a binge eater over there."

Fawn stuck out her tongue, all gooey with chocolate. "So I hear the bitch is back," she said, changing the subject.

"Yeah, and believe it or not, it's actually better this way," Carmen said. "I mean, Mad and I aren't exactly BFFs, but without her, things got kind of boring."

"You should have had me on more," Fawn said. She seemed to think that Madison's absence meant there would be more screen time for her. And she wasn't subtle about it.

"Right, totally," Carmen said, keeping her voice neu-tral. She hadn't told Fawn that the powers-that-be thought she was around too much already. *Lose the shadow,* Trevor had told Carmen. *She doesn't play.* They seemed to like Lily better, but Lily wasn't particularly interested in being in front of a camera. She was more like Drew that way—or like how Drew used to be. Fine being in the background, but not interested in being a main story line.

Anyway, Carmen liked having friends who weren't on the show. It was good to be able to hang out without needing to cover a list of talking points. With no cameras around (except for Lily's iPhone, which was like another appendage), she didn't have to worry about public embarrassment if she spilled a bit of yogurt on her new top, which she'd just done. Oops.

"So I did makeup for Mona Moore yesterday," Lily said, chewing on the end of her straw.

"Oh, I love her talk show," Carmen said as she attempted to wipe up the spot on her top with a napkin.

"Me too. She always has such crazy conversations with her guests. They tell her everything! That one where Gemma Kline basically confessed to being anorexic? That was insane! But FYI, Mona herself is completely *lying* about her age," Lily said. "If she's thirty-five, then my mom's twenty."

"So when she was born, she was already pregnant with you!" Fawn giggled.

Lily nodded. "Exactly."

Carmen savored another bite of yogurt. There was no *way* this was fat-free. "That's totally creepy, Fawn," she said.

"No shit," said Fawn. "So's Gemma Kline. Have you seen that movie where she gets that awful disease and she turns all blue and stuff? I thought it was her best work, but maybe it's because I enjoyed seeing her suffer."

Carmen hadn't seen it. She didn't go to movies that much anymore. She knew she ought to, though. She ought to see what her competition was up to. For instance: What films had the girl who was currently shooting with Luke done? Carmen had no idea.

"So . . . what's up with you lately, Fawn?" she asked. "Any new voice-over work?"

"Oh, I'm keeping busy," Fawn said evasively.

"Faaaawn," Carmen said. She knew Fawn wasn't particularly proud of her voice-over jobs. "Come on. You can tell us. We're friends, remember? *Friends*."

Fawn gazed down at the remains of her yogurt cone. "I taped a tampon commercial," she admitted.

Carmen and Lily both squealed with delight. "Oh my God," Carmen said, "tell me it wasn't the one where, at the end, the tampons all line up and dance the Macarena."

Fawn turned scarlet. She wouldn't look at them. "I plead the Fifth," she said.

Carmen threw her arm around her friend's shoulders. "Hey! Don't *ever* be ashamed of acting work," she said. "(A) it pays, and (B) you're on your way."

"To where, though?" Fawn asked, looking suddenly more vulnerable than Carmen had ever seen her look.

Carmen gave her a squeeze, "To the top, hon," she assured her. "To the top."

Then she grabbed the hands of both of her friends. "We're *all* going nowhere but up. Am I right?"

"Please, God, let her know what she's talking about," Fawn said to the ceiling.

"Nowhere but up," Lily repeated.

Of course, that wasn't what the tabloids were saying about Carmen (and they weren't saying *anything* about Lily or Fawn). This week's exaggeration: WITHOUT HER LEADING

MAN, CARMEN CURTIS IN ROMANTIC FREE FALL. The headline was a pun on Luke's new movie, in which he played a World War II parachutist. The cover showed a photograph of Luke Kelly and his hot new costar looking very cozy (it was for a scene so it didn't bother Carmen) and next to it was a photo of Carmen talking on the phone, looking depressed. She knew exactly when it was taken—she'd seen the paparazzo lurking behind a newspaper stand. And she'd looked that way because she was listening to an old friend's breakup story.

I'm looking sympathetic *in that shot, you idiots!* she wanted to yell. *Not depressed!*

It was really, really annoying. But by this point, Carmen was almost used to the mix of half truths and blatant lies. Sure, *D-lish* had gotten her lunch order right the other day—CARMEN CURTIS LOVES THE EGGPLANT PIZZA AT LAUREL HARDWARE!—but what about their claim that she'd gained five pounds in Luke's absence? (It was only two!) And the bits about how "Little CC" and "indie darling Kate Hayes" are having "tense times"—that really bummed her out. How did they know?

On the bright side, at least they hadn't mentioned anything about her interest in Scientology—something she'd jokingly mentioned to Fawn (who'd been so absorbed in selecting lipsticks at Sephora that she'd probably taken Carmen seriously).

"I'm so glad I have friends like you guys," Carmen

said now. "Let's hit Maxfield's and burn off some of these calories with shopping."

"I thought you were going to your parents' house," Lily said.

"Later," Carmen said. "First, I'm going to spend a month's rent on shoes."

When Carmen got to her parents' front door that evening, she paused and wondered if she should knock. Sure, she had a key—but she didn't live here anymore.

She rang the doorbell, and a moment later her mother was standing in the doorway, backlit in golden light from the hall chandelier.

Cassandra laughed gaily. "Come in, you *goose*, and never ring the doorbell again. Doorbells are for canvassers and Jehovah's Witnesses."

"Uh, I forgot my key," Carmen said.

She didn't want to make her mother feel bad. Now that they'd made up (even if the tabloids were continuing to report otherwise), she was careful not to make things weird between them again. They'd had lunch a couple times since their fight, but tonight was the first time Carmen had been back to her childhood home.

"I hope you're hungry," Cassandra said. "I've got a *giant* chicken in the oven."

Carmen followed her into the spotless white kitchen, fragrant with garlic and rosemary and lemon. She closed her eyes and breathed in deeply. Having a place to call her own was great in a lot of ways, but the kitchen she shared with Kate never smelled like anything but burnt coffee or takeout.

Compared to her Topanga Canyon home, living in her Park Towers apartment felt like living in a hotel. One lacking room service and a maid.

Carmen swiped an olive and a cherry tomato and popped them both in her mouth at the same time, one salty and the other sweet. "Where's Dad?"

"Stuck in traffic. He'll be here soon." Cassandra emptied a container of arugula into a big wooden salad bowl. "So, what've you been up to lately?"

"Well, we're filming the second season, but other than that, I'm sort of taking a break. Figuring out what to do next. What about you?"

Cassandra shrugged. "Not much. A Stevie Nicks tribute concert at Club Nokia. That'll be nice. I like playing the smaller clubs. Reminds me of when I was starting out." She slid a baguette toward Carmen. "Would you slice this for me?"

Carmen obeyed, and then whisked a quick vinaigrette for the salad without being asked. Her mother always put too much garlic in her salad dressing.

"How's Luke?" Cassandra asked as she rummaged through a drawer. "Where *is* that meat thermometer?" she muttered.

"He's good. I think." Carmen paused. "We talked the

other day, but what with the time difference and the long shooting hours—"

"Distance can make keeping in touch difficult," Cassandra said.

Carmen nodded. She missed Luke a lot, actually, and she wished she knew if it was more than she ought to. Things were so . . . *unstated* between them. Was he thinking about her as much as she was thinking about him? There was no way to know.

Unless, of course, she simply came out and asked him. But she didn't have the guts. How ironic: In the role of Julia Capsen, Carmen swears her undying love to him. But as herself, she couldn't ask if she was his girlfriend. "Well, I'm sure things will work out between you two," her mother said with a smile.

That was Cassandra: always the optimist.

Of course, it was also possible that she simply wanted to change the subject. Because when Carmen made a vague noise of assent, Cassandra launched into some long story about a feud between two of their neighbors that had ended with one of them taking a golf club to the other one's vintage Corvette.

The chicken was done and resting on the counter, and Carmen had heard more about her neighbors than she ever cared to know, when Philip Curtis burst in through the back door.

"Smells delicious in here," he said. He gave Cassandra a kiss that lasted a bit too long for Carmen's taste, and then came over and grabbed Carmen in a bear hug. "I've missed you, CC," he said into her hair.

Carmen hugged her dad back. "I missed you, too," she said. "You big oaf."

He put his hands on his ample belly. "I'll have you know that I've lost two and a half pounds in the last month," he said.

"Careful, Dad, you might waste away," Carmen teased.

"I *know*," he said. "Hurry, let's sit down and eat."

At the table, Philip raised his glass in the same toast he'd been making for as long as Carmen could remember. "A toast to my amazing wife and daughter. May they remain forever beautiful and never grow tired of me."

"Never," said Cassandra, beaming at him.

"Where's Drew?" Philip asked, turning to Carmen. "I thought he'd be here."

Carmen sliced into her chicken. "I believe he's spending the evening surgically reattaching himself to my roommate," she said.

"Oh! Well then," Philip said. He took a sip of wine. "I guess we're the ones who'll have all the fun."

Cassandra smiled gently at her daughter. "Does it bother you?"

"No," Carmen said breezily. "I'm super happy for him."

This was about ten percent true. Maybe twenty on a good day. Her mother's glance suggested that she might understand this. But thankfully, she didn't press the issue.

Carmen leaned back against the leather cushion of her chair. It was so *nice* to be home. The rooms were big and beautifully decorated. The couches were soft and draped with cashmere throws. Her bathroom was still stocked with her favorite beauty products, and her childhood bed, with its pale blue quilt and pristine white sheets, was upstairs, practically begging for her to crawl into it.

Oh, and the chicken her mother had made tasted even better than it smelled. Even with all of L.A.'s finest restaurants minutes from her doorstep, Carmen would choose her mother's cooking every time.

She remembered how Madison had moved in with her father but pretended to still live with Gaby. Could she do that? Live here in Topanga, where the air smelled like lavender and eucalyptus and the refrigerator was always stocked with organic salads? Everything would be so much *easier.*

"So, you guys," she said, sparingly buttering a slice of baguette. "I was thinking about my . . . living arrangements."

"Oh, I'm glad you brought that up," Cassandra said. "Your father and I have been talking about it."

They're going to invite me back home, Carmen thought happily. *That is so fantastic, because I am really sick of Sushi Express.*

Cassandra beamed at her. (She was doing a *lot* of beaming tonight, wasn't she?) "We are so proud of you for living on your own. You're learning so much—more than you even know. Remember that both your father and I left home at *seventeen*."

"Yeah, yeah, and you fell in love when you were twenty-one," Carmen said. She knew the whole gooey, romantic story and she didn't need to hear it again. She wanted to get to the part where her mom told her she should move back in.

"Anyway, we think that it's exactly the right thing for you at this time in your life," Cassandra said. "As much as we miss you, we feel that it's important for you to be independent."

Carmen, surprised, looked toward her father. He nodded.

"Independence," he said. "It's one of the greatest gifts a parent can give his child." He paused to spear a piece of chicken. "Besides good looks. But your mother handled that, didn't she?" He mugged for her, but Carmen couldn't smile.

She felt like she was having trouble breathing. But she wouldn't let them see that. "Sure," she said. "Of course. That's totally what I was thinking."

She was too proud to ask them about taking the block off the credit card. She'd have to suck it up. Which meant she'd probably need to take back those Rick Owens boots she bought with Lily and Fawn a mere three hours ago.

It was ironic, Carmen thought. You spent your whole childhood wanting to be a grown-up, and then when you became one, you wished your parents would just keep on taking care of you.

And when they refused? Well, you were on your own.

She thought back to her afternoon with Fawn and Lily and felt grateful to them all over again. Thank goodness she had friends to count on.

8

WHOEVER SAID DREAMS CAN'T COME TRUE

Kate gazed out the window of Todd P. Barrows's office in downtown L.A. She could see the Staples Center in the near distance, its red lights flickering in the misty, late January rain.

"Carrie Underwood played there the other night," Todd said, appearing over her shoulder. "Didn't quite sell out, though."

Kate turned around to face her new manager. "How *could* you sell that place out? It must seat, like, fifteen thousand people." She couldn't imagine ever playing somewhere like that.

"Try twenty," Todd said, steering her over to a chair on the opposite side of his desk.

Kate felt too agitated to sit, but she knew she needed to give PopTV "the most felicitous camera angle," as Stephen Marsh had put it. So she sat down before he could send her a bossy text. (Kate found the new producer totally annoying, and couldn't for the life of her understand why Sophia thought he was cute. Sometimes she wondered if the feeling was mutual—though she was pretty sure that was a wedding band on Stephen's finger.)

Drew was seated in the chair next to her, looking oddly relaxed. He smiled at Kate, and she knew that if she were capable of being calmed down, Drew would be the one to do it. He'd brought her breakfast in bed that morning—Froot Loops, of course—and he'd offered his opinions on all nine outfits she'd nervously tried on, attempting to find the right mix of perky and punk. (Luke *never* would have had the patience for that: Drew was The Best.)

"Can I get you some water?" Todd asked. "Tea? Coffee?"

Kate shook her head so quickly it hurt her brain. She really needed to chill. "No thanks."

Todd smiled. "Don't be so anxious. It's not like you've never been here before. Also, Drew—tell her about the beverage rule."

Kate raised her eyebrows. Beverage rule?

Drew grinned. "Basically, anytime you take a meeting with someone, they're going to offer you something to drink. And you should always say yes, even if you have no intention of drinking it. It's polite."

"That's right," Todd said, nodding. "We have interns whose entire job description is Beverage Fetching."

Kate looked back and forth between them. She couldn't tell if they were kidding or not, and she didn't want to be a dope and ask. Todd was gazing at her expectantly.

"Um, I'll have a water?" she said.

He clapped his hands. "Excellent," he said. He pressed a button on his phone and told the voice that answered to bring him three bottles of Pellegrino. "So," he said, leaning back in his chair. "Now we can begin. Rumor has it you've got a new song I should hear."

Kate nodded as she pulled Lucinda from her case. *Keep calm*, she reminded herself. *This is an audience of two.* Well, plus the PopTV camera crew, but she was used to them by now.

She'd already warmed up in the parking lot outside, so she dove right into the song. A melodic, catchy intro, and then the words: *"I never had a day like this / I dreamed about a kiss like this / Whoever said dreams can't come true / Has never met someone like you . . ."*

Out of the corner of her eye, she saw Drew tapping his foot. Todd's face, though, was blank.

"All the things I should have said / When I woke up next to you in bed / They didn't matter anymore / Just hold me close and lock the door . . ."

When she was done, she set Lucinda back in her case and took two deep breaths before she looked up at her manager.

His expression was dark. He hit a button on his phone. "Hello? The Pellegrino?" he demanded. Then he turned to Kate and smiled. "That was great," he said. "Smart, sassy, poppy. Perfect."

As his words sunk in, she felt her phone buzz beside her in the chair. NICE WORK, Stephen had texted, thereby breaking Laurel's rule against unnecessary texts during shooting.

"Yes," Todd went on, "I've got some good news for you, Kate."

"You do?" Her heart fluttered hopefully in her chest.

"We're going to have you do a showcase. You've got a handful of great new songs, so you're ready for it. We're going to give the labels who've expressed interest a chance to see what you can do. Up close and personal."

Kate sucked in her breath. "Wow, that's amazing. I think? I guess I don't actually know what a showcase means, but it sounds good." She glanced over at Drew. His expression was unreadable.

"That's what I'm here to tell you," Todd said. He snatched the waters from the flustered-looking intern who'd finally come in, and then he explained the concept of the showcase.

Kate's mind whirled as she listened. Todd's management company would rent a fancy rehearsal room, complete with an engineer and a full stage. They would invite A&R executives from various labels, and Kate would perform two or three songs for each group of executives. And, to hear Todd tell it, by the end of the day, she'd have a record deal.

"That sounds . . . terrifying," Kate said. She didn't want to be ungrateful, but "terrifying" actually didn't even come *close* to describing how it sounded.

"It is," Drew said. He sounded grave. "I've sat on those couches, watching bands perform."

"You're going to be great," Todd said.

Kate looked to Drew. She wanted to believe Todd, but Drew *knew* her. He understood how she still struggled with stage fright. Even though she had come a long way, she still wasn't always comfortable in front of a crowd.

"What do you think?" she asked him. "Does that sound good?"

Drew gazed out the window for a moment and then turned back to her. "Sure, it's one way to do it. But there are other ways."

"Like what?" Kate asked.

He shrugged. "I mean, personally? I think you should keep playing around town and building up your confidence. And I think you should have another handful of songs. You should have more of a demo album. Something to send to the A&R guys."

Todd exhaled loudly. "So it can sit in a stack of four million other demo albums? No, they need to see Kate. I mean, look at her! Those blue eyes! That smile! They're going to love her."

Kate flushed. "I don't know about that," she said, then gave a nervous giggle.

"Well, you can think on it," Todd said, looking pointedly and perhaps somewhat angrily at Drew, "but don't think too long. In this business you have to strike while the iron's hot!"

"I know," Kate said. "I'd hate to miss my chance, but I also want to do this right. It's what I've always wanted."

Todd said to Drew, "See? Looks *and* brains. I mean, come on, Drew, *you* think she's the bee's knees. Why won't everyone else? Don't hide her light under a bushel. Remember: Nothing ventured, nothing gained."

Kate wondered if Todd was going to bust out any more clichés. Apparently, Drew had the same thought.

"I'm more the 'a bird in the hand is worth two in the bush' type," he said. "She has solid interest from two mid-sized labels. I don't know that she should chase them off by going after the big guns with a showcase. But Kate, the decision is yours. Just remember, you only get one chance at a first impression."

Kate bit her lip and knocked her toes against the leg of Todd's desk. Should she do the showcase? Take the risk?

Her phone buzzed again. YES YES YES, Stephen had written.

Of course PopTV would want her to agree to it—a showcase would make for a much more exciting story line. They probably already had the space scouted and cleared.

She could almost imagine Trevor rubbing his hands together in excitement. Either she'd do great and get signed to a record label, which would majorly raise her profile—or else she'd utterly bomb, and then Trevor could make it a centerpiece of a "heartbreaking, bittersweet" (or some other BS) episode of *The Fame Game*.

She knew she owed it to her producers to say yes. She

owed it to herself to do what was right for her career.

She stared down at her feet in their new Belle by Sigerson Morrison booties. Why should those things be mutually exclusive? If Todd said she was ready, shouldn't she listen to him? That was what she was paying him for, after all. As amazing as Drew had been, he was just an intern. He still had a lot to learn about the music business. They both did.

She set her jaw. This was her career. Her life. She couldn't keep sitting on the sidelines. "I say we go for it."

She smiled at her decision and turned to Drew.

He looked significantly less pleased.

9

THE NATURE OF THE BUSINESS

Carmen fished a leather Gucci key chain from the bottom of her oversized purse and let herself into Luke's cozy Venice bungalow. Then she dropped down on the worn olive-green couch and exhaled a sigh of relief. She was blissfully *alone*.

She hadn't exactly jumped at the opportunity to keep an eye on Luke's house while he was filming abroad. Even though she really liked him, and kind of owed him for letting her crash there, she didn't like the idea of driving all that way to visit an empty house. (If he'd been lying in bed, waiting for her—that would have been a different story.) But back then Carmen hadn't known that she'd be living with a couple who were currently in the most annoyingly lovey stage of their relationship, either. So in a way, Luke's house had become something of a refuge.

Earlier that afternoon, when Drew came in after class and went straight to the refrigerator as if he had stocked it himself, and when Kate had hurried in and wrapped herself around Drew as if she hadn't seen him in weeks, Carmen piped up and said: *See ya! Gotta check on Luke's!*

So here she was, grateful for silence and solitude.

Missing Luke. Wondering how the filming was going, and if he was thinking about her as much as she was thinking about him. . . .

And wondering if she could live *here* instead of at her parents', while pretending to still live with Kate and Drew. Was there any way Trevor would go for it? If not, could she hide it from him? There was no way he could know where she was all the time. (Though with the caravan of paparazzi that routinely followed her each day he'd quickly catch on.)

Carmen got up and poured herself a glass of water in the kitchen, and then gave some to the potted succulents by the sink (miniature jade plants, a cactus with a strange red protrusion on top, and a sad-looking aloe). She remembered eating breakfast with Luke as the sun poured in through the window. How he'd smile at her, all sleepy and rumpled. How the air held the delicious smell of coffee, and how sometimes the ocean breeze came whistling through the eaves. And how she'd smile back at him, still a little bit shy, and the next thing she knew he'd be pulling her onto his lap, his warm hands finding the buttons on her shirt. . . .

Carmen took a gulp of water. Those were the days, she thought, and she wished they could have lasted longer. Maybe the two of them could have figured out what was going on between them. As things stood now, they weren't boyfriend and girlfriend, but they weren't *not* boyfriend and girlfriend. They were in a weird Limbo Land, which was a fine enough place to be when they were both on the same continent, but it got lonely with him thousands of miles away.

She knew it was good for Luke's career, but she really wished he hadn't booked that part last minute and jetted halfway across the world.

For the next *three months*.

Maybe part of the problem was that she didn't have anything to do with herself lately. Not that filming *The Fame Game* wasn't work—it was—but there was nothing else on her iCal but lunch dates and salon appointments. She'd gotten used to the crazy hours of movie shoots, and now that she wasn't on set, the days seemed long and empty. Especially with Luke gone, and with Krew in her face all the time.

But she wasn't ready to dive into another project, especially because she wasn't finding the perfect Next Thing. She'd turned down a role in a romantic comedy because she'd hated the director's previous movie, as well as a part in an animated feature because she felt it was too small. After all, she'd just starred in a guaranteed blockbuster. No more supporting roles for this girl.

These were, to use her mother's term, "Champagne problems." Problems someone like Fawn would kill to have. Which was why Carmen didn't talk to her about them much: Fawn would try to be supportive and understanding, but as a person whose most recent job was the voice-over for an embarrassing tampon commercial, there would be limits to her sympathy. Carmen could imagine her staring in disbelief: *You turned down a role in an Actual Movie?* she'd shriek.

Carmen sighed. Sometimes it seemed to her like the only pure, uncomplicated friendship she'd ever had was with Drew.

Carmen watched as the water she'd poured into the jade made a puddle on the counter. How much H_2O did these things need? She wished Luke had left her instructions.

Of course, she could easily call him, couldn't she? Hearing his voice might make her feel better. And maybe then his plants would stand a better chance of surviving.

She got out her phone and clicked his number in Face-Time. In a moment, Luke's giant eyeball appeared on her screen.

"Ahh!" she yelped.

Luke cackled and pulled his phone back so that she could see his whole handsome face, in a touch of movie makeup. "Sorry about that," he said, not sounding sorry at all.

"I hope you don't answer calls from your agent that way," Carmen said.

"I don't video chat with my agent, love," Luke said. "Do you?"

Carmen shook her head. She'd had her agent ever since *The Long and Winding Road*, but he never seemed to do anything for her at all. Her mom kept telling her she needed a better one, and Carmen knew she was right. She knew, too, that it'd be easy to find a new agent with *The End of Love* coming out—but it was one of those business-y, bureaucratic-type things that she hated to think about. She wished her agent could find her a new agent.

"How's the shoot going?" she asked.

"Good. Sandra Kopp is *way* mellower than Colum McEntire."

"Harvey Weinstein is mellower than Colum McEntire," Carmen said wryly. "I mean, Harvey might shove people out of cabs now and then, but he doesn't threaten to murder them." She turned the phone toward the plants. "Say hi to your freshly watered plants. Do they look okay to you?"

"They look great," Luke said. "You only need to water them like once every two weeks, you know. Now turn the phone back around so I can look at your lovely face."

Carmen flushed and hoped he couldn't see that. "Flatterer," she said softly.

"Flatterer, nothing. That's the truth," Luke said. "I wish I could see you right now. In person."

"Me too." She so wished he'd say, *Hey, I've got a break in shooting. Come for the weekend!* Because she'd hop on that plane immediately, even if it meant more time in the air than it did with Luke. But he didn't say it. And she was too uncertain to suggest it.

"So—how are the ladies?" Luke asked. "Mad still causing trouble? Gaby doing okay?"

Carmen noticed that he didn't ask about Kate. "Everyone's fine," she said. "Madison is back, in case you hadn't heard, and Gaby's out of rehab and so far doing a good job of staying clean." (If Luke didn't ask about Kate, she wasn't going to offer anything. No use in opening *that* can of worms.)

"What about you? I read that you're totally *pining* for me, going *mad* with longing. I think I saw a blurry picture of you looking forlorn. . . ." He snickered.

Carmen wanted to bang her head against a wall. Luke was halfway around the world—shouldn't he be out of *D-lish* range? "Ugh, it's so freaking annoying! I mean, I do miss you, of course. But I did *not* gain weight, by the way, in case you read that part."

Luke waved it all away. "Don't worry, love. No one takes any of it seriously."

"I know. It's so tiresome, though."

"But it's the nature of the business, isn't it?"

"I don't recall reading about any forlorn looks or weight gain on your end. Just photos of you and your pretty new costar."

Luke shrugged. "People don't pay as much attention to my figure because it's not as nice as yours," he said, ignoring the mention of his costar.

Carmen flushed for the second time.

"Well, love," Luke said, "I have to run. They're setting up my shot. Talk soon?"

She nodded.

He blew her a kiss, and she blew one back, and then he was gone.

"Nothing ever gets *stated*, you know?" Carmen said. She and Lily were walking along the Venice boardwalk, past the T-shirt shops and pizza joints, past the buskers and sunburned hippies and tattooed punks. Carmen sort of hated the boardwalk, but both she and Lily had been in the neighborhood.

Lily nodded. "It was like that with this guy I was dating. Actually, I don't know if we were dating or just hooking up. See? It's been *over* for six months, and I still don't know what it was exactly."

Carmen smiled. "Maybe we should come up with a questionnaire. You can hand it to the guy at the end of the date, like one of those restaurant comment cards. 'Your experience tonight was (a) an official date; (b) hangin' out; (c) the first step to marriage, eternal happiness, et cetera; or (d) the price I gotta pay to get a little action.'"

"Brilliant," Lily laughed. "It would solve everything."

"Except that if I gave one to Luke he'd be like, 'Huh? What's this, love?'" Carmen said in her best attempt at an Australian accent.

"Because he's British he can say 'love' without precisely meaning it."

"He's from Australia, actually. I'm surprised he doesn't call me 'mate.'" Carmen's tone was slightly rueful. The conversation with Luke had been less reassuring than she'd hoped.

Lily stopped at a rack of sunglasses and slipped on a bright turquoise pair straight out of the 1980s. "Here," she said, holding out a set of mirrored frames. "See how they look on you."

Carmen shook her head. "I don't need to put them on to know. They'll look *terrible*."

Then she noticed the salesgirl staring at her and motioning to the cashier guy to look, too. Carmen averted her eyes. She was definitely used to being recognized, but today she didn't want to be. She reached out and grabbed a black baseball cap pinned to the wall. "Here," she said suddenly, handing Lily a twenty. "Do you mind buying this?"

When Lily returned, wearing a pair of knock-off Wayfarers she'd purchased for herself, Carmen donned her black cap.

"Incognito!" Carmen said happily. "Now no one will write in to *D-Lish*: 'Carmen Curtis seen *not giving money* to sad, homeless guy on Venice Boardwalk!'"

Lily said, "Now you can be as bad or as good as you want to be. In *disguise*." She nudged Carmen playfully with her elbow. "Not to say that you're ever bad, of course."

"Of course not. But how fun: I can eat an ice cream without reading about how I'm stress-eating. So—should we or shouldn't we?"

They were right near Venice Beach Ice Cream now, with its cute courtyard and green-tiled roof. Inside there was gelato practically begging to be eaten.

"I always say yes to ice cream," Lily said.

When they emerged a few moments later, licking salted caramel cones, they agreed that ice cream was a thousand times better than fro-yo, and the next time they met up with Fawn, they should definitely go for the good stuff, calories be damned.

"I should have asked for sprinkles, too," Lily said. "My ice cream looks so naked. But anyway. Back to this Luke business. Are you sure things are really so up in the air? I mean, maybe he assumes you guys are together. You were living together, after all."

"That was a matter of necessity," Carmen said. "One could argue that I was using him for his couch."

She hadn't been, of course; it had been an added bonus (not that she often slept on it). But then for some reason, a headline flashed in her head: *Carmen Curtis and Luke Kelly: Relationship of Convenience?*

There'd be damning evidence for the article; after all, they'd been "dating" during the movie, and then they'd "broken up"—news that had brought them, and the movie, loads of publicity. Then, only a few weeks later, they were either dating, or "dating," or being friends with benefits, while she was living with him because she had nowhere else to go. . . .

Lily laughed. "You were *not* using him for his couch,"

she said. "Perhaps for his hot body or those dreamy eyes."

And then Carmen heard herself say: "No, I wasn't using him. But who knows what's up with us? For all I know, he's dating up a storm. I'm keeping my eyes open. I hear Jonah Byrne is newly single."

Lily's mouth dropped open. "Jonah Byrne of Sadly Sarah?"

Carmen nodded. "I met him a few weeks ago, and he gave me his number."

It wasn't as if she'd actually *planned* to lie to Lily, but talking to Luke had reminded her of his last-season advice to plant fake information with her friends and contacts. And almost unconsciously, it had just happened. Maybe she should lie to a few others in her circle now, and then sit back and see if and when she read about it.

10

LARGER THAN LIFE

Madison never thought she'd miss Laurel, but this new producer of Trevor's had made her reconsider. Stephen Marsh was simultaneously bossy and unsure of himself, and he wore T-shirts with the strangest slogans on them. (TRUE INTENTIONS—what did that even mean?) Madison was waiting to make her entrance to Cabbage Patch for her lunch with Sophie, but Stephen kept stalling: First the lighting wasn't right, then he didn't like the look of the waiter that had been cleared to serve them, and it took half an hour for the restaurant to provide them with another.

Madison, who had been in the middle of a juicy *Vanity Fair* article about the rise and fall of a certain Hollywood action star, wished she had stayed longer on her chaise longue. She couldn't help it; she sent Trevor a text: YOUR NEW PRO-DUCER NEEDS TO GET HIS SHIT TOGETHER. AMATEUR!

Luckily for Stephen, he was working with the new and improved Madison—while she wasn't inclined to actually *help* the guy, at least she had no plans to cause professional trouble for him (one of her old specialties).

"Stephen, you know I have a hard out at one, right?" Madison said impatiently over the producer's shoulder.

"The schedule says we have you until two. It's almost one now. We can't shoot an entire lunch in fifteen minutes." Stephen turned back to the camera operator he was talking to.

"Stephen," Madison said a little louder. "I have an event at five, and I have to get into hair and makeup. Sorry, but it's part of my job." She shrugged.

Stephen looked more than a little irritated. "Actually, Madison, *this* is your job. You're free to attend as many boutique openings and fragrance launches as you want in your spare time, but when you've been scheduled to film, I expect you to be here. And I expect you to have a better attitude."

Madison seethed; *no one* spoke to her that way, especially not some clueless producer and in front of the whole crew. Who did he think he was? This was her show, not his. And if she felt at *all* like being old Madison for a moment, he'd be lucky to produce a Taco Bell commercial by the time she was done with him.

But since fighting with him might result in the shoot going even longer, she held her tongue. For now.

A moment later she was cleared to go, and the camera followed her through the restaurant as she met Sophie at a corner table. Madison was smiling, of course, but inside she was still angry: Stephen was a buffoon, and Trevor had insisted on this sisterly meet-up instead of filming Madison later this evening at the club they had cleared. Madison needed a better foil for her fabulousness than Sophie, or some wannabe actor that Trevor had decided looked good on camera. But how would that work? Who would it be? She'd have to ponder it.

"Namaste," Madison said as she got to the table—only so Sophie wouldn't.

"Hey, sis," Sophie said. She stood to hug her, but Madison, almost imperceptibly, shook her head. It was fine to have lunch with her sister and play reasonably nice on camera, but there was really no need to go overboard.

Madison sat and crossed her legs delicately at the ankle. She was wearing a white Calvin Klein sheath dress—very chic, very *grown-up*—and strappy gold sandals. (She'd guessed, correctly, that her sister would be in some vivid maxi-dress monstrosity, and she'd wanted to offer a contrast.)

"Nice dress," Sophie said. "Don't order a Bloody Mary."

"Nice dress," said Madison. "Don't suffocate in all that polyester."

Then, for a moment, they merely smiled at each other. Love-hate in their eyes, with maybe a slight emphasis on the latter.

Then Sophie reached across the table and patted Madison's hand. "Seriously, it's so good to see you. You were gone on vacation for so long—I thought you might never come back."

"It *was* great," Madison said. "But of course I had business interests to attend to."

Sophie raised an eyebrow. "New endorsements?"

"Oh," Madison said breezily, "let's not talk about work. Let's order." The fact was, she didn't have any deals on the horizon, though she was pestering Nick, her agent, to come up with something (*anything*). Sophie probably knew this, too, and was hoping she'd get Madison to admit it on camera. (She wouldn't.)

The waiter appeared the moment Madison raised her index finger. "Ladies," he said smoothly, "Good afternoon. Can I tell you about today's specials?"

"Two tuna tartares and two house salads," Madison said, cutting him off. "Please."

"And a Cajun rib eye," Sophie said.

Madison shot her a look. Last she heard, Sophie didn't eat mammals.

"It's for Jay," Sophie explained. "He'll be here any second."

Madison rolled her eyes and didn't bother hiding it from the camera. "Why?" she asked.

"Why not? I think he's funny," Sophie said.

"He's an idiot," Madison responded. (She *really* hoped Trevor would keep that line.)

"Everyone else likes him," Sophie said.

Madison knew she wasn't referring to their fellow cast members; Sophie meant that the *Fame Game* viewers loved him. According to Trevor, they thought Jay was hilarious.

They found him good-looking, too. ("Parking-lot hot," Carmen called him—because he looked like the kind of bad boy who hung out in the high school parking lot, smoking instead of going to class.)

No, the only people who loved Jay were the ones who didn't have to be in the same room with him. Were *The Fame Game* an elimination show, Madison would have done everything in her power to get him kicked off a long time ago.

"You should have warned me," Madison said. "I'd have brought my . . . actually, I probably wouldn't have showed up."

"I know, that's why I didn't tell you," Sophie said pointedly. "Besides, it could be worse. At least I didn't bring Dad this time."

Madison sucked in her breath. Even more than six months later, she could still feel the shock of seeing her father for the first time since she was nine, when Sophie hauled him along to their lunch date at Barney Greengrass. *Surprise! It's our long-lost, deadbeat dad!*

It had been a crazy few months that followed that emotional ambush, full of ups and downs that eventually landed Madison in a courtroom committing perjury. For a while, Madison had felt part of a real family. But where was Charlie Wardell now? No one knew. Madison had gotten one stupid postcard—and then nothing.

"Look," Sophie said, "here comes that cutie now."

Madison turned and saw Jay galumphing toward them,

a button-down thrown over his tank top and jeans so low and baggy they barely covered his boxers. She couldn't *believe* she was going to be subjected to him. He was even worse than one of her horrible Trevor-supplied dates.

"Greetings, beautiful ladies," he said. He gave Sophie a kiss, then leaned into Madison but she ducked it.

"You order for me, babe?" Jay asked.

"'Babe'?" Madison repeated, wondering if Jay was enough of an idiot to try to date two girls on the same TV show at the same time. (Gaby had finally copped to hooking up with Jay again. "I can't help it. I like him soooo much," she'd said.)

Jay laughed as he scooted his chair in toward the table. "Oh, not 'babe' like *that*," he said. "Not *my* babe. Just *a* babe."

Sophie beamed at him. Madison understood that it wasn't because Sophie found him charming, either, although Sophie might pretend otherwise. Madison knew her sister, and her sister was absolutely not that stupid. (She was, however, potentially stupid enough to make a move on that idiot Stephen Marsh. Not that Sophie had said anything, but Madison had seen the look Sophie gave him when she first arrived. . . .)

No, Sophie was sucking up to Jay because of his audience popularity. Ever since she'd figured out that her peace-and-love trip did little to make her appealing to the fans, she'd been looking for another angle. Madison could understand that; after all, she was looking for a new angle herself.

As far as Sophie was concerned, Madison would have advised her to lose the tent dresses and the yoga act, but hey, she wasn't her sister's manager.

The waiter returned to ask Jay if he wanted a drink. "You got a Heineken, playa?" Jay asked.

Madison's eyes widened. *He did* not *just call the waiter "playa,"* she thought.

But actually he had, and he called him "son" later, and finally, to cap it all off, "homes." Madison felt like crawling under the table. *Anything* to be away from Jay.

Except, of course, the cameras were rolling and she ought to stay in their line of sight. (She had to keep her story line #1.)

"So—do you remember how Kate told us she'd waited on Gemma Kline at Stecco?" Madison asked. "Well, I happened to be in a dressing room next to her the other day, and I overheard her and her assistant talking about how her assistant got, like, a flesh-eating bacteria from a bad manicure."

Sophie's brow furrowed. "Is this really lunch-time conversation?" she asked.

"Of course! So then I was looking at *D-Lish* and it had this picture of Gemma and her assistant—who, by the way, is totally going to pull a Kim K and bypass her former boss, you can tell—and it said: *Gemma K and Annie B visit*

Dr. Bloom for celebrity microdermabrasion. And I'm like, Yeah, right: Try a major dose of antibiotics and the name of a personal-injury lawyer."

"Oh, Mad," Sophie said. "You're so funny. I've really missed you, you know."

Sophie looked very earnest when she said this, but Madison wasn't buying it. "Really."

"Of course! I think we should hang out more. I think we should hang out all the time! We're sisters, Mad. We share a bond that's both earthly and spiritual—"

"Please don't go down the New Age wormhole," Madison interrupted.

"—we have to be there for each other. We have to support each other in what we want to do and how we want to live, and we have to—"

Madison stopped listening and took a bite of her tuna tartare. She understood why Sophie wanted to "hang out more." It was the same reason she wanted to hang out with Jay: because Trevor wouldn't turn the camera on her unless she was with someone viewers liked better.

If she weren't still mad at Sophie, Madison would find her desperation endearing.

What Sophie didn't seem to understand was that you had to be larger than life on TV. You had to laugh louder, and frown deeper, and wear higher heels, and gossip more, and relax less. . . .

It was *acting.*

And it was the kind of acting that Madison excelled

at. As Sophie talked on, and Madison nodded her head, pretending to listen, she realized that this was the sort of helpful information she could share. She wouldn't share *everything* she knew, but she could divulge enough to help someone reach sidekick status. Yes, maybe *this* was the angle she was looking for. . . .

Everyone knew that the lead character of the show was only as good as those who followed her around, hanging on her every word. Maybe Madison had been playing it wrong by keeping her tricks to herself. Maybe it was time to share some of the spotlight—if only to make her own star shine a little brighter.

Not with Sophie, though, because Sophie didn't deserve her help.

With Kate, who Perez Hilton once called "as charismatic as a coatrack."

Madison had sworn not to waste time helping anyone else, but if helping Kate meant helping herself, that didn't count as kindness, did it?

11

THINGS ARE ABOUT TO CHANGE

Kate was curled up in the corner of her couch, sipping a cup of green tea and watching an episode from the first season of *The Fame Game*, which Madison had DVR'd. (Madison saved *every* show, clipped *every* magazine article; one of these days she was going to have to rent a storage space for her archives.)

"Okay," Madison said, "now watch this scene here." For the last half hour, she'd been talking through the scenes like a football coach on the morning after a big game.

The camera focused in on Madison and Sophia, who were sitting at a café in Beverly Hills. TV Madison said, "I think Gaby and Jay are in kind of a weird place in their relationship, but they seem happy." Then she flipped a piece of hair over her shoulder. "But if you ask me," she went on, "she's drinking a lot. Sometimes I feel like things are going to . . . well, *change* for her. . . ."

Real-life Madison hit pause on the remote and turned to Kate expectantly.

"So—wait. What's the part I'm supposed to do?" Kate asked.

When Madison had offered to give her some reality TV pointers, Kate had eagerly agreed. She was tired of being called "boring" and "vanilla" and "ho-hum." But so far she was having a hard time understanding why Madison was apparently so great at TV while she herself was apparently not. Besides the whole camera-hog thing, obviously; she *knew* Madison was better at that.

Madison explained, "You make vague but important-sounding pronouncements. 'I feel like things are going to change for her.' Or 'What could possibly go wrong?' Or 'Everything is going to be different this time.' Those are good because Trevor can use them as teasers in the commercials they play all week long, and as a cliff-hanger at the end of an episode. Which means that your one sentence will get played about a hundred times."

"But it's sort of an unspecific and boring sentence?" Kate said hesitatingly.

"Unspecific, yes. But boring, no. Having your sentence be the tease puts you at the *center* of the drama. The one who's either right—or spectacularly wrong. Which it is doesn't really matter." Madison fast-forwarded as she talked. "As you can see, as far as the Gaby prediction goes, I was correct. Things changed for her all right. She spent a month in lockdown."

Kate reached down and picked up Lucinda as she waited for Madison to find what she was looking for.

She'd promised herself she'd practice six hours a day until the showcase, but she'd only strummed two chords before Madison whirled around.

"*Ahem.* What are you doing?" Madison demanded.

"Um, playing a guitar?"

"Would you play a guitar in calculus class?"

"What? No."

"Well, then put that thing away, because this is a lot more important than calculus. Honestly, you're lucky I'm even taking the time to help you with this."

Kate did as she was told—although it wasn't like playing guitar wasn't important, too. She had the showcase to think about, after all. Wasn't her musical future a bigger deal than whether or not she got the teaser line? "Should I take notes?" she asked, half jokingly.

"Probably," Madison said. She *wasn't* joking.

Kate searched on the coffee table for a pen and paper. Madison enjoyed bossing people around—that was clear—and Kate truly was grateful to her for it. She'd shown a real flair for reinventing people on *Madison's Makeovers*, and now she was sharing her secrets. Kate ought to sit up straight and pay better attention. She would spend some quality time with Lucinda later.

"Ready now, O pupil of mine?" Madison asked.

Kate nodded, smiling. Ever since she realized that the off-camera Madison was nicer than the on-camera one (though she still had an acid tongue), their friendship had blossomed. Kate liked off-camera Madison's sometimes goofy sense of humor and her relaxed sense of fashion. Tonight, for instance, she was wearing a messy ponytail, a soft, faded T-shirt, and a pair of giant fuzzy slippers. It was a side that she'd *never* let *The Fame Game* see, and it was super cute.

"I'm totally ready," Kate said. "Amaze me with your wisdom." She wrote *How to Be* Not *Boring* at the top of her scrap paper.

"All right. Note how, in group scenes, I always keep in view of the camera. I'm never lost in the crowd like some dispensable secondary character. It helps to wear bold colors too. I'm partial to red, but anything that helps you stand out is good. Also, pay close attention to the story lines for each scene. If the scene isn't focused on you, then do everything you can to interact with whoever the producers *are* focusing on."

"Don't you sometimes want to hide, though?" Kate asked. "Don't you get sick of the cameras in your face?"

Madison shook her head. "As *if*. Oh, something I forgot to mention about the Gaby scene: Talk about your castmates on camera. Shows like *The Bachelor* always do cast interviews where everyone bitches about each other. People love that. Think of your one-on-one scenes as an on-camera interview."

"And bitch?" Kate asked doubtfully.

"If you can't find it in your heart to bitch, plain old gossip is sufficient."

Gossip, Kate wrote. *Make predictions*. She looked up at

the TV screen. Sure enough, Madison was at the center of the scene; even at a crowded party, she stood out as if she'd hired a spotlight to stay trained on her.

Madison watched herself for a moment, nodding thoughtfully, and then turned back to Kate. "Wait a moment before answering questions. Look intent. Or thoughtful. Or whatever the scene calls for. Have the appropriate expression on your face, but say nothing for at least three solid seconds. That increases the tension while the audience waits for an answer."

Stare!!! Kate wrote.

She wondered, as she doodled in the margins of a P.F. Chang's menu, if Carmen knew this information instinctively, having grown up around cameras the way she did. Or maybe Cassandra had fed Little CC showbiz advice along with her bowl of morning Cheerios: *Always smile for the cameras, dear, always let them see your brightest self.*

Certainly no one ever compared Carmen's scenes to "watching paint dry." (Though they'd certainly said other nasty things about her. What was the headline the other day—something about Carmen spending $10K on cellulite treatments?)

"Look at yourself," Madison ordered, pointing toward the TV. "See how you're practically vanishing into the wallpaper?"

"Thanks a lot," Kate said.

"You have to lean forward. You can't let that idiot

Jay block you. Remember he's, like, three times as big as you are. And ten times as loud." Madison stopped and looked thoughtfully at the screen. "You know . . . I'm thinking. . . ."

Kate shot her a look. There was something about her tone that made Kate nervous. "You're thinking *what*?"

Madison turned toward her, an excited expression on her face. "One of the main rules of reality TV—and if you don't know this one by now there's *definitely* something wrong with you—is that you aren't yourself on TV. You're a type. A character. You either play the part, or you're edited into it afterward." She clapped her hands together. "God, why didn't I think of it before? You're being a real person on camera, Kate, when everyone knows that real people are boring."

"Hey! I'm getting a *security team* because I have some-one so in love with me that he might pose a threat to my personal safety," Kate said. "So clearly I'm not, like, totally boring."

Madison's eyebrows shot up. "*What?*"

Kate giggled. "I can't believe I didn't tell you. Trevor called this morning. Remember how I was getting those creepy fan letters? Well, Trevor—or his lawyers, maybe—decided that I needed to have a security detail. Because they think the guy could be some kind of threat or something."

For a few beats, Madison was quiet, seemingly shocked. Then she composed herself and said brusquely, "You're basing the level of interest you have on this show on the obsession of a crazy person?"

Kate bit her lip. She was slightly hurt that Madison wasn't more concerned for her safety. "I don't know why they don't take out a restraining order," she said.

"Because that would only call attention to him," Madison said. "And for all we know, that's what he wants."

It seemed crazy to Kate. She pictured the Park Towers hallway full of Secret Service men in gray suits and earpieces. Cameras in the elevator. A tracking device she'd carry in her purse. It was so James Bond. And it wasn't like she was actually scared of J.B. from Studio City. (Though her mother would have told her to be, which was why she hadn't shared details of her current situation with her family.) Kate was more . . . confused.

Kate narrowed her eyes at Madison. "You're not a tiny bit *jealous*, are you?" She smiled. "Because having a rabid fan is kind of flattering."

Madison scoffed. "Please. I don't look for ego boosts from crazy people."

"He might not be *crazy*," Kate said.

"Of course he is," Madison said. Then she smirked. "If he was sane, he'd be stalking me."

Kate stuck her tongue out at her friend, and when that didn't seem like enough, she gave her a shove with her foot.

Madison laughed. "The point is, though, you don't need to worry about him. Especially not if you've got security. So let's get back to the discussion at hand."

"Which was . . . ?"

"*Types.* Wake up, girl. I know you're staying up late writing songs for that showcase thing and loving on Drew, but this is important. Do you think Gaby is as ditzy as she acts?"

"Um . . . yes?" Kate didn't want to be rude, but the evidence was pretty strong.

"Well, believe it or not, she isn't. I mean, she's no genius. But she's not the box of rocks you and everyone else might think."

Kate was definitely taken aback by this news. "She doesn't seem that different off camera, though. She's still pretty ditzy."

Madison waved this away. "She just forgets to stop acting. Like Christian Bale stays in character the whole time he's filming something. He doesn't even give interviews in his own accent. He's *always performing.*" Then she shrugged. "Oh, and Gaby was on pills for the last year, so there was that."

Gaby and Academy Award–winner Christian Bale? That was a comparison Kate never thought she'd hear. "You're sort of blowing my mind here, Mad."

Madison laughed. "We have to get you a character, Kate. And your character is obvious. I'm the bitch, Gaby's the ditz, Carm's the Hollywood royalty, and you, my dear, are the *rocker.*"

"I mostly play acoustic," Kate pointed out.

"You know what I mean. Here's the thing. We have to get you a new look." Madison reached out and grabbed the end of one strawberry-blond lock. "We have to cut this off and bleach it. *Platinum*."

Kate felt her heart start beating harder at even the mention of such a thing. She'd had long hair ever since she was four (except for a brief period at age six, when an unfortunate encounter with bubble gum ended with her mother giving her a sloppy bob with kitchen shears). Also: *platinum*? Like Lady Gaga? Like Christina Aguilera? Like Punk Miley Cyrus?

"You'll look like such a badass," Madison said. "Like a *rocker*."

"Don't you think Trevor would mind?" Kate asked, touching her head protectively. She didn't want to sound like a coward, so she blamed her hesitation on him.

Madison scoffed. "Please. It's your hair. I'm sure he'd love it if you shook things up a little. Anyway, he doesn't own you."

"Well, he sort of owns everything around me," Kate said, thinking of the apartment and the furniture and the new electric guitar, etc.

"Actually he rents," Madison pointed out. "So. Do you want to go to Rick Roberts or Kristin Ess' Salon? Kristin is *amazing* at color, and her place is much more discreet. You don't want to be photographed leaving the salon. The new hair should be a surprise."

"I don't know about this idea—"

Madison patted Kate's knee. "It's brilliant. Trust me. This is what I do best."

Kate thought about it for a minute. Madison *was* a professional when it came to makeovers—or had been, anyway. And while some people might have reasons not to trust Madison's motives, Kate didn't have one at the moment.

"You pick," she said. She felt brave and tough and bold.

"It'll be a whole new you."

"I wonder what Drew will think."

"He's going to love you no matter what, that's what he'll think." Madison paused. "He's a good guy. You're lucky to have him." Her voice was soft and vaguely wistful.

Kate could tell that Madison's thoughts had shifted away from haircuts and toward Ryan Tucker. Madison had given Kate the rundown of their relationship back when she was recovering from her lipo. Their story was a perfect rom-com script. Well, almost. *Boy meets girl, boy hates girl, boy comes to love girl. . . .* But then: *Boy leaves girl.* That sort of screwed up the expected happy ending.

Madison maintained that their breakup was for the best, but Kate wondered if she actually believed that.

"So—no promising specimens on Trevor's guy reels?" Kate asked.

Madison shook her head no. "He's looking for another Jay. Some jerk in an Affliction T-shirt and questionable facial hair that all of teenage America will inexplicably fall in love with."

Kate laughed. "It's a tough life," she said.

"He texted me, you know," Madison said suddenly.

"Who?"

"Ryan."

Kate sat up straight. "*And?*"

Madison sighed. "I didn't text him back yet. He says we should talk. That he still cares about me."

"That's not surprising," Kate said gently. "It sounded like you guys really had something."

Madison picked at the silk fringe on a throw pillow, seemingly lost in thought. "What's the point? What's good for me professionally doesn't necessarily fit with what's good for me personally. Although—who am I kidding? The guy broke my heart, Kate—as much as it's possible to break it." Here she offered her trademark Madison smile. (But was that a slight tremor in the corner of her mouth? A hint of vulnerability?) "So maybe he's not good for me personally, either."

Kate nodded understandingly. She wished she'd actually met Ryan so that she could offer her own piece of advice. But he was like some mythical creature: There were plenty of stories about him, but no actual sightings.

"I think you should text him back," she said. "You're in a stronger place now. Maybe you can have it all."

Madison smiled. "Oh, I'm going to have it all," she said. "But I'm still working on exactly what 'it' is."

"I hear you. Hey, maybe that's your theme song." Kate picked up the guitar again and plucked a few notes.

"Sometimes I'm your therapist / Sometimes I'm just a bitch / Do I want love or stardom / I really don't know which . . ."

Madison, laughing, threw a pillow at her but missed.

Kate couldn't help herself. *"I'm on a show called* The Fame Game */ Can't throw a pillow cuz I got bad aim—"*

Then Madison, squealing, picked up another pillow. This one was a direct hit.

12

AN ENTIRELY DIFFERENT PERSON

At first Trevor hadn't recognized her. Who was that platinum blonde with the pixie cut talking to Carmen— another one of Carm's hair-and-makeup pals? Someone (hopefully) more interesting than Fawn and more telegenic than Lily?

Then the blonde had smiled a familiar smile, and Trevor had done a giant double take. That little creature, that punk-rock *elf*, was none other than his own Kate Hayes.

He'd about fallen out of his chair. *Why* hadn't anyone warned him? It should have been the first thing he heard about the moment the crew showed up to shoot. But Stephen Marsh was apparently still too new to the job to figure that out. Or too stupid, or too intimidated, or something. Either the man lacked common sense or balls. Trevor wasn't sure which was worse.

Now he got up and tossed a few punches at the speed

bag he'd had installed in the corner of his office. (He'd gotten into boxing lately; it was fantastic stress relief.) Kate's new hair was going to cause a major continuity problem.

To make a good episode of *The Fame Game*, Trevor relied on being able to comb through hours upon hours of scenes from different days—different *weeks*, even—and edit them down, shaping them into what was essentially a one-hour highlight reel, built around whatever theme or story line he'd chosen to focus on that week.

For instance, he had a decent dinner party scene from a few days ago that lacked resolution; the Carmen-and-Kate tête-à-tête he'd just watched would have been the *perfect* scene to attach at the end, since they'd dished about both Madison and Sophia. But he couldn't use it, because Kate *looked like an entirely different person.*

He had to wonder: Did Kate lack all common sense, too? She was usually so predictable. Wherever had she gotten the idea to transform herself into this new Kate? A look that was, by the way, less than one hundred percent flattering. She suddenly reminded him of a Bratz doll.

As Trevor began to breathe harder, sending bare knuckles again and again toward the speed bag, the realization came to him. *Madison Parker.*

Of course it had been her idea—he was sure of it. She was thumbing her nose at him again. Reminding him of her ability to cause trouble.

He hit the bag harder. Madison's disappearance had

already caused him huge continuity problems. Once she agreed to come back, he'd assumed he'd no longer have such issues. But apparently Madison had decided to show him how wrong he was.

To make the next few episodes work, he was going to have to pull some major Frankenstein action: cutting here, splicing there. . . . There would have to be some hats and hairpieces involved, too.

He turned and went back to his desk and sank into his chair. It gave him a migraine to even think about it.

He called Laurel. "We're going to do logs," he said brusquely. "I want a log and photos of *every single item* of clothing and *every* accessory the girls wear to a shoot, so if we need pickup scenes we'll have that information immediately. I even want their *nail* polish colors written down. This is their job, damn it. I'm not playing around." He bent a paper clip in two, then pitched it toward the trash. "On second thought, I want the girls to pick a specific color of nail polish and stick with it for the remainder of the shoot. There will be no haircuts. No dye jobs. No visits to Dr. Botox. No more elective procedures until this season wraps. Make that clear to them."

Laurel assured him she would.

"Gaby especially," he added.

"I'm on it," Laurel said, and clicked off.

Trevor wondered if he ought to make Kate get extensions and dye her hair back to its original color. Then he could film her getting it re-cut and re-dyed. Or else he could make her wear the extensions for the next few months and hope that no one noticed. . . .

He wondered why, when his more volatile stars finally seemed to be behaving themselves—Gaby staying sober, Madison doing what he asked (with the exception of the Kate makeover)—his supposed Midwestern Good Girl had to go and screw things up.

And while it wasn't her fault she'd picked up a stalker, the security team was costing the production a pretty penny.

He sighed. It was also inconvenient. The camera crew was used to shooting around Kate's absurd mess, but how were they also going to avoid the burly guys hired to hang around her apartment to protect her?

If Trevor hadn't sent Kate back to Ohio mere months ago, he would have certainly done it again. He drummed his fingers on the desk, imagining it. Maybe he'd send Carmen with her, so the two of them could play out their best-frenemy drama on a different stage. He laughed, imagining Carmen's reaction to a flat landscape of soybean fields and strip malls, where the best restaurant around was a tie between Chili's and the Olive Garden. . . .

It was unfortunate he couldn't make everything he wanted happen. But all in all, Trevor Lord knew he wasn't doing too badly, and he had the fat year-end bonus and a new Lamborghini to prove it.

And every week, as reliable as his delivery of *Variety*, Trevor was sure to open a tabloid and see an item on one or more of his girls. If that wasn't winning the Fame Game, then he didn't know what was.

13

A REGULAR CUPID

Carmen was supposed to meet Laurel at her favorite nail salon on Beverly Boulevard, but at the last minute Laurel changed her mind; apparently she'd seen something about flesh-eating bacteria and manicures and was feeling very anti-salon.

So they rendezvoused at a new boutique on 3rd Street instead, and as Carmen flipped through a rack of fluttery tunics and skinny jeans, Laurel slipped her feet in and out of various pairs of pumps, mules, and ankle boots.

"Do you remember Anna Baker from high school?" Laurel asked as she admired a pair of Proenza Schouler booties. "She got a DUI last night after sideswiping a cop car in an In-N-Out Burger parking lot."

"Ouch," Carmen said. Anna Baker had been a senior when Carmen was a freshman. She was one of the popular girls: By seventeen she'd already starred in two dumb but profitable teen rom-coms. "Was that on TMZ?"

"Actually her mom ran into mine at yoga in

Brentwood," Laurel said. "TMZ's got nothing on the maternal grapevine."

"Too bad my mom's not part of that. She actually gets her gossip from blogs, so she's wrong half the time. But that sucks for Anna—though it seems like everyone has a DUI these days," Carmen noted.

"Yeah—if you weren't already in the tabloids so much, I'd suggest you get one for the sake of the publicity."

"My dad would *kill* me," Carmen said, holding up a butter-yellow smocklike garment. "He's still not over Tank-topgate." The color was lovely, she thought—it reminded her of spring sunshine. "What do you think of this?"

Laurel shook her head firmly. "Uh-uh. Looks like an apron a kindergarten teacher would wear so she doesn't get finger paint on her clothes."

Carmen put it back on the rack. Okay, so the yellow smock was a miss. She selected another shirt, held it up, and got another no from Laurel. Her third shirt pick prompted Laurel to make a gagging face.

"Girl, do you need eyeglasses?" Laurel asked.

Carmen felt herself blushing. This was *bad*. She hadn't shopped in ages, ever since her parents cut her ties to the family bank account. (She'd even returned those beautiful boots she'd bought with Fawn and Lily.) Was shopping like spinning class—you had to keep doing it or else you lost your edge? Or was it possible she'd lost her sense of taste? No. Not possible. She must be overtired.

"Here," Laurel said, handing Carmen a sleek dress of

copper-colored silk. "Try this one on. It'll bring out your eyes."

Carmen did as she was told. She could see Laurel's feet under the dressing-room door, pacing back and forth. She wondered if she should hire a stylist to go with her new publicist. (She'd shared Sam at Beckwith Associates with her mother for years—but when she and Cassandra had their fight, Carmen hired Sam's colleague, Lacey Gilmore.) A stylist could probably get Carmen more free clothes than she was already getting, which, considering her parents' credit line was off-limits indefinitely, was a real plus. (Had she really blown most of her earnings on fantastic clothes, to-die-for handbags, and a new silver Range Rover? Why yes, it seemed she had!) Carmen made a mental note to do some stylist investigation.

"We need to talk about your story arc," Laurel called through the door.

Carmen zipped up the dress, opened the door, and gave a twirl. "What do you think?"

"Love it," Laurel said, but her mind was clearly on business now. Which was why she was an executive producer at twenty-three, or however old she was. Laurel's *life* was PopTV. (And her wardrobe proved it—how old were those Seven jeans anyway? Laurel ought to be trying on a few things, too.)

Carmen, on the other hand, believed in a balance between life and career, which was why she wasn't rushing out to take another project. "Do you guys have some plan for me?" she asked, adjusting the dress's belt.

Laurel shrugged. "I wouldn't go so far as to call it a *plan*. But we do have a suggestion." She handed Carmen another dress, this one slightly more structured and in a deep jade green. "We think you need to find another project sooner rather than later. Preferably high profile, but not too time-consuming. Maybe a rom-com? We didn't have enough access to you during *The End of Love*, and Trevor didn't like that."

"Isn't my project filming your show?" Carmen asked.

"I think you know the answer to that question," Laurel said. "That green'll look really good on camera, too."

Carmen nodded; of course she knew the answer. *The Fame Game* was about four girls trying to make it in Hollywood—not about two girls trying to make it, one girl trying not to accidentally kill herself, and one girl who sat around and pondered what to do next with her life. The problem was, she still hadn't come across any projects that interested her. The only thing that had seemed remotely appealing lately was a *play*, but Trevor had nixed that idea immediately. "Plays are for theater nerds. Movies are for stars," he'd informed her. "You, Carmen Curtis, are a star, and don't you forget it."

Of course there were *hundreds* of A-listers who acted in plays (Cate Blanchett! Nicole Kidman! Katie Holmes!), but Trevor still wouldn't hear of it.

"So you think I should take the role in that stupid Vegas heist movie?" Carmen asked Laurel.

"The one starring Vince Otto?" The producer shuddered. "No. That guy is a pig. He'll spend the whole time trying to sleep with you."

"Which would be fine with you guys, I'm sure, as long as he'd be on the show," Carmen said, half joking.

Laurel grinned. "Yeah, I'm sure Trevor wouldn't mind. But honestly, Carm, there are a million great roles out there."

"Funny, I haven't seen any of them," she muttered, zipping herself into the green dress. She turned this way and that in the mirror; she liked it, but she had the feeling that her mother had one very similar. "I can call my agent," she offered. "See if he's holding out on me."

"Sure. And if he's got nothing, there are other options to spice up your arc, too."

Carmen put her own clothes back on and walked up to the register with the first dress she had tried on and her credit card. One perk of not shopping: She was nowhere near her limit. "I'm listening," she said.

Laurel smiled brightly. "Romance," she said.

Carmen raised an eyebrow at her, then signed the receipt and tucked her new dress under her arm. "*Romance? Really?*"

"Look, your boyfriend—who won't film anyway—is out of town," Laurel began, heading for the exit.

"He's not exactly my boyfriend," Carmen said. She wished she could say otherwise, but . . . well, all the hours they spent on FaceTime somehow hadn't resulted in any official status updates.

"Perfect, then," Laurel said. "We'll get you and Madison going on double blind dates, and—"

"What are my other options?" Carmen interrupted. She wasn't sure which sounded worse: going out with a bunch of would-be actors or spending extra time with Madison Parker. Also, while she and Luke weren't officially together, she was pretty sure he wouldn't appreciate her filming a series of dinner dates.

Laurel sighed as she held the door for Carmen. "It really would be the easiest one," she said. "It'd make Trevor happy. He loves romance."

"Yeah, he's a regular Cupid," Carmen said.

"If you don't want a dating arc, then you should pick a fight with Kate or Madison, or do *something* to create conflict. Because if you don't? You're just the background for other people's stories, Carm. The sounding board."

Carmen was taken aback by Laurel's frankness. "Wow," she said. "Okay. Thanks. Message received."

"Or we could bring in the whole tabloid thing—how there are these weird stories about you all the time. . . ."

Carmen shook her head quickly. "No, I hate thinking about it."

"It'd be *great* TV, though," Laurel said. "There'd be this big sense of mystery. . . . Does your publicity camp have a leak? Does some blogger have it in for you? Are you really addicted to pistachio ice cream? Do you really not know how to pump your own gas? Et cetera."

Laurel sounded so excited by this prospect that Carmen

looked at her sharply. It would be *totally* unethical for Laurel to have talked to the tabloids about Carmen in order to stir up drama for the show—but would she, for the sake of her job? Carmen tried to think if there was anything she'd told Laurel that she'd later read about online. . . .

They were outside now, and the hazy January sky made the colors of the world seem bright and harsh. Carmen reached into her bag for her sunglasses. She told herself that it couldn't be Laurel. But where did the blame lie?

Laurel squinted at her. "You started this game with a leg up on everyone else, thanks to your family, Carmen," she said. "I'm sure you don't love hearing that from me—you've heard it your whole life—but it's true and you know it. But so what? No one ever said life is fair, and frankly, I don't want to see you lose your advantage."

Carmen nodded grimly. She got it. She'd been sitting on the bench the last few weeks; it was time to do a better job of playing the game.

After walking up and down 3rd Street, wondering what drama she could create, getting belatedly offended by Laurel's lack of tact, and picking up a few paps along the way, Carmen spent nearly an hour sitting in traffic on Sunset. By the time she pushed open her front door, she was ready for peace, quiet, and a very long bubble bath. She prayed the apartment was empty or—at the very least—that Drew wasn't around. She simply wasn't in the mood for . . . well, for anything but solitude.

So when she nearly tripped over a tanned, muscular guy wearing pleated chinos and a black shirt with SOCAL SECURITY embroidered on the pocket, she let fly a very long and impressive volley of curse words.

The guy, who was in his mid-twenties, with green eyes and a deep cleft in his chin, said, "Sorry about that, mama."

Carmen ignored the apology. "Who are you?" she demanded.

He stood up (he'd been viewing a laptop that was displaying a video feed of their front door) and held out his hand for her to shake. Carmen pretended not to see it. She was normally a polite person, but this particular moment was an exception. She blamed it on the traffic. (And maybe a little bit on Laurel.)

"Rick Hales," he said. "Personal security expert."

Carmen's first thought was that he had come because of her. She was the famous one, after all, and she'd grown up around security teams thanks to Cassandra's superstardom. (Cassandra had had more than her share of crazy fans.) And what with all the negative ink the tabloids ran on her, she certainly seemed to have an enemy. "Why are you—" she began.

"We've been hired by PopTV to keep an eye on your roommate," Rick said. "Seems she's been getting a number of questionable letters. I don't want to worry you, of course, but the network did feel that she—and you—would be better off with some extra security."

Carmen felt like screaming at the top of her lungs. All

this giant hassle was because of *Kate*? But instead she leaned against the cool taupe surface. "So I guess you're going to be hanging around the apartment all the time now," she said, sounding less than thrilled.

When Carmen was little, she hadn't been able to tell all the beefy security guys apart. Also, she thought they'd been hired as her playmates. She couldn't understand why they never wanted to color in her coloring book or play Barbies with her.

"I prefer the term 'monitor,'" Rick said.

"Oh, okay, because a different *verb* makes it less of a hassle," Carmen said, tossing her bag on the floor and stepping around him.

Kate was in the kitchen, nodding as another security guy—this one older and wearing a suit—explained the guards' schedule to her. She looked up and smiled at Carmen, brushing her new and startlingly platinum bangs away from her forehead.

Her expression was slightly embarrassed. But it seemed to Carmen that there was also a twinkle of pride in Kate's pretty blue eyes. She was clearly loving this.

"Hey," she said, sounding breathless. "This is kind of insane, right?"

Carmen opened the refrigerator and scanned the contents. Wasn't there a tube of Toll House batter she could devour? Why wasn't there anything but ketchup, peanut butter, and packets of soy sauce in the fridge? "Um, yeah, kinda," she said.

It was annoying enough to have *one* guy living in her apartment, and now there were going to be a dozen others. She wouldn't be able to walk around the living room in her nightgown anymore, or leave her clean bras dangling from the shower rod. She'd be too embarrassed to do her yoga and she would now never, *ever* be alone.

If there was any silver lining to this, it was that Kate might stop leaving her dirty laundry and old magazines and candy wrappers all over the apartment.

Her phone buzzed; it was Fawn calling. Carmen sighed and picked up.

"Hey, girl," Fawn cried gaily. "I'm in your 'hood. Can I swing by?"

"It's kind of hectic over here at the moment—" Carmen began.

"Are you throwing a party or something?" Fawn asked. "Without me?"

"Hardly—"

"Well, good. I'll come over and make it a party." And then she hung up.

Carmen opened the fridge again, as if some delicious treat would have miraculously appeared in it. But sadly: no.

When Fawn arrived, mere moments later, her eyes grew wide. "Who are these guys and where did you get them?" she whispered. "They are *hot*."

"It's Kate's new security team," Carmen said. She flopped onto the couch and closed her eyes. "Personally, I don't know why we couldn't have gotten a Rottweiler or given her some pepper spray. This feels a little dramatic."

Fawn cackled. "Because why would you want a dog when you could have a hunk? Excuse me, I'll be right back."

Then Carmen heard her introducing herself to Rick, and after that, the high giggle of her laughter. Fawn was such a *flirt*.

Carmen felt the cushions sink down beside her. Reluctantly she opened her eyes. Kate was right there, biting her lip.

"The Boring One is really sorry," she said.

Carmen was still annoyed, but she tried not to be for Kate's sake. It wasn't her fault, after all. She had a beautiful voice and a sweet personality—of course people would love her, some to unreasonable degrees. "You're not boring," she said. "You're *trouble*."

Then she smiled, and Kate smiled back. Still friends.

14

THE TIME OF MY LIFE

The red velvet ropes parted and a smattering of cameras flashed as Madison and Gaby approached the entrance to Blok. Gaby smiled and waved, but Madison gave a single, coy over-the-shoulder glance. Five paparazzi were there, and by now Madison practically knew them by name.

Gaby teetered in her stilettos and reached out to Madison to steady herself as they stepped into the dim room, eyes still adjusting from the flashes. Gaby hated being so short, which was why she always wore such ridiculously high heels. Madison dreaded the day Gaby learned about surgery to lengthen shinbones. As awful as that sounded, she was sure Gaby would jump at the chance.

The PopTV camera followed them as they entered the loud club. Madison sighed immediately, because she knew that every word she spoke tonight would be unintelligible and would have to be dubbed over in a sound booth. There went half her Saturday.

The girls made their way to the table in the VIP

section, where another camera was already set up and recording the two guys they'd come to meet: Jay and . . . *whatshisface*? Madison almost laughed; she'd already forgotten her date's name. All the dating reels she'd watched had blurred together. Was he Connor? Trey? Paul? Well, this was clearly going to go *great*.

He was blond and handsome (like most of the guys Trevor and Laurel had dug up; there'd been a few brunets and one authentically ugly, rich dude), and he stood as they approached the table, smiling. "Hey, I'm Drake," he said, and then leaned in, forcing her into an awkward half-hug.

"Nice to meet you," Madison said, thinking, *Drake? Is that his real name or his stage name?*

"Totally," he said, nodding happily. "I'm so stoked."

Stoked. Well, that was a bad sign.

Jay called out a greeting, which Madison ignored. He slung his arm around Gaby and said, "I missed you, babe."

Gaby fluttered her eyes at him. "I missed you, too," she whispered, snuggling up against him.

Madison knew she could live to be a thousand years old and she'd still never understand what Gaby saw in Jay. She was reaching for the bottle of Dom, but Drake stopped her. "Allow me," he said, expertly filling her flute.

He must be a bartender, Madison thought. She wondered why Trevor never found her an actual professional. Someone who was already something, instead of still trying to *become* something. A lawyer, say—or maybe a dermatologist, because it'd be nice to get a friends-and-family discount on her next microdermabrasion. . . .

Of course, she knew why these people were never options on her dating reels. They would be too old. Too serious. Too unlikely to show up to a party in shorts and combat boots, or to crack lewd jokes, or to try to belch the entire alphabet—all things that fan-favorite Jay specialized in.

"Babe, I brought you something," Jay said, his voice artificially loud. He handed Gaby a small velvet bag.

Gaby nearly squealed with delight. "What is it? Is it jewelry?"

Jay thrust his chin out. "Open it," he said, his voice proud.

Madison and Drake watched as Gaby clawed at the bag, and eventually pulled out . . . a spark plug.

Gaby frowned. "What is it?"

Jay grinned, obviously pleased with himself. "It's a spark plug, babe."

Gaby looked at him in confusion. "What am I supposed to do with it?"

"Nothing! It's, like . . . how do you say it? It's a symbol." He reached out and took it from her. Then he held it up above the table, as if they were all supposed to admire it. "The spark plug, see, is part of the internal combustion engine. Without it, the engine won't run. And so here's the cool part. Like, the internal combustion engine is my heart, right? And you're the spark plug. If I don't have you, I don't work."

"You *don't* work," Madison said. But Jay didn't hear her.

Gaby held her hands up to her reddening cheeks. "Oh, Jay, babe, that is so sweet."

Madison eyed the bottom of her empty glass. Wow, where had all her Champagne gone so quickly? She reached for the bottle again and glanced over at Gaby: That *was* seltzer she was drinking, wasn't it?

Madison turned to Drake. "Do you have a screwdriver to give me or something? Maybe a socket wrench?"

"Uh . . ." Drake patted his pockets, and after a moment produced a packet of wintergreen Life Savers. "Um, okay. So these Life Savers are my *very* special gift to you. They are symbolic of our relationship, which began approximately five minutes ago. Without you, Madison, my breath would never have such minty freshness."

Madison laughed and helped herself to a Life Saver. It was possible that Drake wouldn't turn out to be such an awful date after all, which would be nice. Besides, thanks to Jay, the companion bar hadn't been set very high. And then maybe she and Drake could go on a second date—not because she thought she'd actually *like* him, but because she'd like a break from meeting guys for the first time on camera and having to pretend like she was enjoying herself. At this point she'd given up on compatible. She'd settle for tolerable.

(Because if she couldn't have Ryan—and she couldn't— what was the point?)

Gaby had the spark plug back and was stroking it like

a pet. "Isn't Jay sweet?" she asked Madison, her dark eyes shining.

Jay knocked back a glass of amber liquid and cleared his throat. He began to address the table (and by extension, the cameras). "I've been thinking about how, like, your feelings have no mass, or energy, or whatever, but they totally control what you do, right? It's like they only exist in your mind. But no one's going to tell you that they're not totally real. Which is why I don't care when scientists say that ghosts are only in your mind, because that doesn't make them not real. Just because something's in your mind doesn't make it fake or made up. Do you know what I mean?"

Madison had no idea what to say. Why on earth had Jay started talking about ghosts?

But Gaby nodded. "*I* know what you mean," she said. "Science is all in your mind, too, right? Like numbers and things. But numbers are totally real."

Jay said, "Yeah. Ghosts and numbers, man, ghosts and numbers."

Madison could feel the camera focusing in on her for a reaction shot, and she knew she was expected to look dumbfounded. (Which, actually, she was.) She widened her eyes, and then let a tiny smirk play in the corners of her mouth.

Drake leaned forward. "Are they serious?" he asked.

Madison nodded. "Oh yes," she said. "Unfortunately."

Drake looked over at them as if wondering what

stupidity they'd think of next. "Do you want to dance or something?" he asked.

Madison turned around to scope out the small dance floor. It was mostly empty still, though the retro disco balls sparkled and spun while the DJ played catchy mashups.

"No thanks," Madison said, offering Drake a small, apologetic smile. "Not right now." She hadn't been to this club before and she was starting to suspect it was lame. Who'd scouted this location—that idiot new producer, Stephen Marsh? She really had to do something about him. . . .

"Okay, negatory on the dancing," Drake said, shrugging. "Maybe later."

He looked a little nervous, Madison thought. Of *course* he wanted the date to go well. If it did, they'd go on another one, and maybe he'd have a shot at being a regular. Like Jay. And then he could quit his bartending job.

Madison missed Ryan with a sharp pang right then. He was about the only person in her life who she *knew* wasn't using her for fame. In fact, he wanted nothing to do with her fame.

Not that Ryan was really in her life at the moment. But they'd finally talked the other night, when Madison made the mistake of answering her phone without looking to see who was calling. (She *did* want to hear Ryan's voice, but she'd decided it was better if she didn't—so until that particular fumble, quick texts had been their only means of contact.)

He'd told her that he missed her, and that all the animals at Lost Paws still missed her, too. His sisters had asked about her, he said, and when he and his mom had had lunch at Rosa's Café, he'd thought of the date they'd had there.

"Sometimes I wonder if we made a mistake," he'd said. "Do you ever think that?"

Madison had managed to dodge the question. For one thing, there was no "we" to discuss: *He* was the one who'd broken up with her, so if there had been a mistake, he'd been the one who made it. For another, she still wasn't really sure how she felt.

Ryan was saying all the right things to her. How good he'd felt when he was around her. How he still wanted to call her twenty times a day. But Charlie had said all the right things to Madison, too, and look how well *that* turned out. He'd abandoned her all over again. Who was to say Ryan wouldn't do the same thing?

Drake reached out and lightly touched her arm. "You all right?" he asked.

Madison nodded. "Of course. What are the rocket scientists talking about now?"

Jay leaned forward across the table and tapped Madison's wrist. "Mad, you look mad," he said. "Get it? Mad's mad?"

She rolled her eyes and pulled her arm away. "I'm having the time of my life, Jay. Can't you tell?"

Jay shook his head earnestly, apparently incapable of picking up on sarcasm. "Not really. You know, it's like I'm always telling Gaby. Your mind is your most powerful organ, right? And it can totally control your emotions. So let's pretend you're not having fun, because right now you are. You can be, like, 'Mind, you better shape up,' and poof! it will. Your mind is the boss of your mind, if you know what I mean."

"Wow," Madison said. "I've never heard such profundities."

"Now, I don't know what that word means," Jay said, "but I'm just saying, you can be happy if you want to, Madison."

She felt herself stiffen. Was there actually some truth to what Jay said? Was she capable of not worrying so much about her father if she simply *decided not to*? She didn't want to ponder that now. "I am happy," she snapped. "I am ecstatic, in fact." She reached over and grabbed Drake's hand. "Come on," she said. "Let's dance."

The cameraman lumbered after them, and she knew that anything she and Drake might say would be incomprehensible thanks to the thumping bass. Well, whatever, Trevor could throw in subtitles or not, she didn't care. Right now she needed a break. Even if it meant dancing in public.

She smiled at Drake, relieved to be away from Jay and glad that for a moment, conversation wasn't necessary. He misread her look as flirting and put his arms around her waist, and ever so delicately—politely even—Madison removed them. She tossed her hair and gave a little hip shake.

Drake was a nice guy; he really was. He probably looked good on camera, too, and maybe they'd date some more if Trevor asked her nicely. And if he agreed to reinstate the white flowers provision in her rider (not because she cared about alabaster peonies—because she cared about winning). But Madison didn't want Drake getting the wrong idea. He would do, but he was no Ryan Tucker. Her body and her heart were both off-limits.

15

SPICING UP A STORY LINE

Carmen, wearing the coppery silk dress Laurel had picked out for her and a pair of Giuseppes (from last year, but still fabulous), eyed the raucous party from the balcony above. She'd braved the crowds around the wet bar, and then picked her way through knots of girls in tight dresses and guys in fitted deep-V's before deciding to step away from it all. The place was a total meat market, and while Laurel would obviously love it if Carmen found someone to flirt with, Carmen wasn't feeling it.

Although, considering what she'd read about her "roving eye" on *D-Lish* this morning, she'd probably be accused of flirting with any guy she happened to walk past.

It was tiresome, but Carmen could handle lies like this—they were just part of being famous. What bothered her far more than being called "boy crazy" was her suspicion that she had finally figured out the identity of the blog's source. Too bad Carmen had invited her to the party before that particular lightbulb switched on.

"Hey, Carm," Sophia yelled, gesturing for her to come down. Sophia had on some sort of Pocahontas costume: beads, a bikini top, and a fringed leather skirt. If anyone on *The Fame Game* needed a stylist, Carmen thought, it was *that* chick.

Carmen shook her head and pointed toward the stairs, as if they were simply too difficult to climb down at this particular moment. Sophia shrugged and immediately turned her attention to some guy with a long, gelled-back ponytail. She was an even bigger man-eater than her sister. Carmen had even heard rumors that Sophia was hooking up with someone in PopTV production, but she couldn't summon the energy to care who. Besides it wouldn't be the first time someone hooked up with a crew member.

Carmen knew that Kate and Madison had gone out to the pool area, where the hosts had set up tents strung with white lights and clusters of tables, as if the event were an upscale wedding instead of an enormous rager. Gaby, who seemed pretty tipsy (red flag!), was out there somewhere with Jay, and Fawn had texted a while ago to say that she and Lily had arrived and they were in search of some friend from high school that Fawn was dying for Carmen to meet.

Carmen, who'd learned a thing or two about avoiding parties thanks to early experiences at her parents' house, had simply swiped a nearly full bottle of wine from an end table and brought it along with her upstairs, and now she was over halfway done with it. She was doing a terrible job of spicing up her story line at the moment, but she just needed a minute or two away from the spotlight.

She told herself that by the time she got a little further into the chardonnay, she'd feel inspired. She just hoped the producers wouldn't find her before then. She knew Laurel was somewhere in the crowd searching for her; she'd gotten the text. But Laurel could play Find Carmen a little bit longer.

"Look at you, up here all by your lonesome," Drew said, appearing by her side. He eyed the wine bottle. "Drinking alone?"

"Not anymore," she said with a smile.

He settled in beside her and took a sip of his Sierra Nevada. She noticed a patch of gauze on his arm, right below his elbow.

"Did you get *another* tattoo?"

He nodded. "A bass clef."

"Nerd," she said affectionately, giving him a gentle poke in the ribs with her elbow. It was nice to see him. By himself. (When was the last time she'd seen him without Kate secured to his side?)

"I'm a nerd like Flea's a nerd."

Carmen frowned. "Who's Flea?"

Drew looked shocked. "Oh, only the bassist for a minor band called the Red Hot Chili Peppers. You might have heard of them?"

Carmen shrugged. "Never liked them that much," she said.

"Well, he's great. And bassists—"

"Are the unsung heroes of rock 'n' roll, I know," Carmen said. Her dad had an entire speech about Paul McCartney's bass playing, but Carmen very rarely listened to it. "So, where's your other half?" she asked. Just to be polite.

"She and Madison had some deep secrets to discuss on camera or something," he said.

"Madison's probably giving her the numbers of all her plastic surgeons," Carmen said.

Drew pulled back. "Whoa," he said. "Kate would never."

"Well, she did just bleach her hair almost white," Carmen pointed out. "So you never know."

"That's a totally different thing," Drew said. "And she looks great."

"I know, I know," Carmen said. "But Mad is all about surgical enhancements, in case her bra size doesn't make that blatantly obvious."

"Didn't I see an item about *you* getting something done?" Drew said. He grinned and squeezed his pecs suggestively.

Carmen was *so over* people bringing up things they'd read about her online or in *Gossip*. But she kept her tone light. "That was last month's news, Drew. But, no, I didn't, in case you had any doubts. You should know, you practically live in my apartment." Then she bit her lip, wondering if she should go on. Should she talk to Drew about her suspicions? She knew that he didn't like being in the middle of a conflict. But he was her best friend, even if they didn't spend that much time together these days, and wouldn't he want to know? How she'd seen something she'd really hoped she wouldn't?

Besides the whole boy-crazy accusation, *D-Lish* had quoted "a source close to the actress" saying that she "definitely isn't pining for Luke Kelly. In fact, she says she's keeping her dating options wide open, and she might have her eye on a certain hot young rocker."

It was *exactly* what Carmen had said to Lily a few days ago in Venice, but so far she hadn't been able to bring herself to confront her (so-called) friend. She'd talked to Fawn about it, and Fawn had told her to keep the information to herself for a while. "Let's wait and see," Fawn had said. "Honestly, if you confront her she might say more stuff about you. It's better to phase her out."

So Carmen had been quietly worrying about the situation ever since, which might have been why she wasn't really in a party mood.

"So," Drew said. "How's tricks?"

"Remember how Luke told me that I should feed fake information to my friends?" Carmen blurted.

"Yeah. Didn't he want you to say you were considering Scientology? Did you? Because I didn't read that, but I would have liked to. 'Carmen Curtis works to uncover her thetan, the omniscient, non-material core capable of unlimited creativity. . . .'" He snickered.

"It's not funny, Drew," Carmen said. "And it's *weird*

you know their lingo. But anyway, it's annoying to have lies printed about you all the time. Even if they're small ones. What if you saw your picture tomorrow on the web and the caption was like, 'Drew Scott covers up his new One Direction tattoo'?"

He grinned. "Now, that *would* be funny. Can you plant that somewhere, too?"

Carmen drained her glass of wine and sloshed some more in her cup. "The thing is," she said, "I told Lily that I had my eye on someone besides Luke, which of course I *don't*, and it showed up on *D-Lish.*"

"But anyone could have offered up a lie like that. It's too generic."

Carmen shook her head. She was glad that Drew always assumed the best about people, but he couldn't *always* be right. "I gave Lily a name, though. And then I basically see it in print. That's pretty specific. It's always the same writer, too. Like there's some reporter who has it in for me."

"The reporter's only printing what he's being told."

"By Lily," Carmen repeated. "So what I'm thinking is, where there's smoke, there's fire."

Drew grinned his goofy, familiar grin. "And where there's wine, there's a party. Why are you not sharing?"

Carmen handed him the bottle and he took a sip right out of it. For a moment she was annoyed at him—for not taking the gossip thing seriously, and for drinking the wine she had begun to think of as her personal bottle.

But then Drew put his long, tattooed arm around her shoulder. "Oh, CC," he said. (He was the only person not related to her who was allowed to call her that.) "I've missed you. We never hang out anymore."

"I've missed you, too," she said.

She sighed. She was willing to drop the Lily subject. And she wouldn't let herself say *anything* about Drew walking around her apartment in a towel. Or how she had come to refer to him and Kate as Krew. She was only going to focus on the positive.

So she drank her wine and thought about how loyal he had been to her, all through high school. How he had been her chauffeur and protector and confidant. How he'd thrown her a surprise party on her fifteenth birthday, and taught her how to drive a stick shift, and taken her to the prom when her stupid boyfriend dumped her the week before. Drew had always, always been there for her. He was her rock.

But now he was there for Kate.

Carmen felt her spirits sag. She noticed that the edges of the room seemed slightly warped and fuzzy: Either she'd suddenly developed nearsightedness or she was getting a little drunk.

Thank God she wasn't down with the rest of those people, having a camera focusing in on her face. She was so glad to be hiding out with Drew on the balcony, above it all.

"Remember the night my car broke down and you

came to rescue me on PCH?" Carmen asked.

"And then we went down to the beach and sat on the sand—"

"—and it was totally freezing, but you rolled up your pants and went in anyway—" she said, feeling better already.

Drew threw back his head and laughed. "—and then when I splashed you and you got so mad at me, and then you made me buy you a burger and a shake at Mel's Diner even though it was, like, two a.m. by then—"

"—and my parents about *killed* me when I came in the door, but when I told them I was with you they weren't mad anymore. And they made us hot cocoa and we all sat in the kitchen and talked. . . ." She was almost giddy, remembering.

It occurred to Carmen in that moment that being friends with Drew was one of the few decisions she'd ever made that her dad hadn't questioned.

Drew had loved her so much then. Why hadn't she ever loved him back?

She felt achingly nostalgic for the time before all this, when they were inseparable. And then nostalgia made her suddenly wild and reckless. "Drew," she said softly. He turned to her, the smile still on his face. And she leaned toward him and kissed him on the mouth.

Almost immediately, he recoiled.

"Whoa, Carmen," he said, backing away from her. "What are you doing?"

Her heart was hammering in her chest. She had no idea what to say.

He held his hand over his lips. "You *kissed* me," he said.

As if she didn't know that! "Oh my God, I'm sorry," she said, instantly full of regret. "I don't know what I was thinking. I *wasn't* thinking."

Drew was shaking his head. "It's really weird," he said. He looked at her sternly. "And totally inappropriate."

She wanted to crawl under the Turkish kilim rug covering the polished wood floor. Or dive over the railing into the party below.

Drew stood up abruptly. "I think I should go," he said.

Carmen didn't say anything at all. She only nodded. And then she watched him walk away and disappear into the crowd.

She could only hope he wouldn't tell Kate. She could trust him, couldn't she? He wouldn't want to cause conflict between the two of them, especially now that they lived together. He knew Trevor loved fights and he wouldn't give him the pleasure of airing one.

Carmen had managed to convince herself that it was no big deal—no harm, no foul—when she put her hand on the waistband of her dress and felt something.

Her mike pack.

It was still on and recording every word.

16

BIGGER. BETTER. BRIGHTER.

Kate had been up past 2 a.m. every night lately, rehearsing for her upcoming showcase, and she had the dull skin and under-eye bags to prove it. She'd tweaked a couple of older songs, giving them much better hooks, and written two and a half new ones. (Not that the half did her much good.)

Todd, her manager, seemed very pleased with what he called Acoustic Kate, but he insisted they visit a production studio "for some musical experimentation." Which was how she came to find herself in a mixing room at Studio Nineteen early on a Sunday morning, shaking hands with Johnny and Adam, two engineers, while casting nervous looks at Drew, whom she'd brought along for moral support.

Todd gave Johnny the digital files of Kate's songs, and he made quick work of transferring them while Adam brought Kate and Drew bottles of Evian. (Kate didn't want hers, but after remembering Todd's instructions had taken it anyway.)

Suddenly Kate's voice came over the monitors as she sang about "Los Angeles, that delirious dream." She was startled by the volume, by the clarity of tone. She could hear how Lucinda had not been perfectly tuned. Oops.

Todd nodded as he listened. Adam and Johnny were expressionless, though, and Kate ached to know what they were thinking. Did they like it? Hate it? She'd been standing in the corner, fidgeting, but now she felt like her legs were going to give out so she walked over to the leather couch and sank down. It was huge and black, and so soft she felt as if it might swallow her completely.

She reached for Drew's hand and nervously traced the vine tattoo on his wrist. She didn't look up again until her song had ended.

Johnny, to her great relief, was smiling. "Yeah, this is going to be good," he said. "I think we need to experiment with the sound a little, though. Get something a bit bigger and more polished. Poppier."

Drew leaned forward. "More polished?" he said. "But don't you think the raw quality of her voice and her guitar is part of its appeal?"

Johnny shrugged. "Well, yes, but—"

"Sure," Adam interrupted. "It's totally awesome if you want to have an audience of dudes in berets who smoke clove cigarettes and girls who wear vintage dresses with combat boots. What we're talking about here is making her a *star*. You can't do that with one poorly tuned acoustic guitar." He turned to Kate. "No offense."

"None taken," she said, which was a lie.

"Let's mess around with it a little," Johnny said. "It'll be fun."

They started by muting her guitar track, so all that was left was her voice, which, when they played it back again, sounded strange and alone.

"All right, I think we need a drum loop—something simple, not too flashy. It'll ground us." Johnny leaned over a computer and poked at some keys.

"Give it some syncopation, though," said Adam.

"We have preprogrammed beats," Johnny explained to Kate. "We've got a ton of stuff right here and ready to go."

Kate nodded. "Okay," she said softly.

The drums came up and she tapped her foot to the beat; it was lively and bright. Playful. It wasn't how she'd imagined her drums—well, actually she'd never really imagined drums. So, whatever. She could go with it.

As Johnny played around with the beat a bit more, Adam went to the keyboard and began to pick out a melody. "Something like this," he said. "Then we'll add a synth bass line. . . ."

Kate watched the engineers as they played a track, shook their heads, and then tried something else. Sometimes Todd offered a few suggestions, but mostly he sat there listening. It was strange to see the process of them picking apart her song; it felt, a little bit, like watching herself be operated on.

"Is this what you want?" Drew whispered.

"What do you mean?" Kate asked.

"Euro-pop sweetness—" she overhead Adam saying.

"The vocal's good," Johnny said. "But we need to strip out her music. Replace it with other music."

Adam nodded. "Let's make it bigger: big breakdowns, buildups, big instrumental parts."

"Yeah, and when she records we'll have to use Auto-Tune," Johnny said. "She pitches sharp sometimes."

"What if we loop the first half?"

"Not sure about the synth chords—"

Kate had absolutely no idea what they were talking about.

"It's like I don't even need to be here," she whispered to Drew.

He nodded grimly. "I know."

"What's the matter?"

Drew shook his head—he didn't want to say. So Kate pressed further. "Tell me. Tell me now."

"They're turning you into someone else, Kate," he said. "You're never going to sound like this in real life. This is all fake."

"But don't they know what they're doing?"

"Sure, if you want to be Katy Perry. But that's not who you are."

Kate thought about the pop star: her colorful wigs, her entourage, her sold-out tours, her songs that people couldn't get out of their heads, even if they wanted to. "It doesn't seem so bad, though," she said. "In fact I like the sound of it."

Drew crossed his arms. "I like *you*. The raw sound of your voice. Lucinda. The way you sometimes miss a note."

"I miss notes?" Kate was surprised.

"Of course. And it's perfect. It's like how screwing up in the first few minutes of an open mic can actually bring an audience over to your side, so by the time you finish your songs they're in love with you."

"I don't want to be loved for my mistakes," Kate said.

"But that's, like, the human condition!" Drew said. "You live, and you screw up, and you try harder, and you love people and they love you back."

"Are you getting metaphysical on me?" Kate asked. "And why are you so obsessed with mistakes today? Did you eat all my Froot Loops again?"

She was trying to lighten the mood a little, but Drew seemed weirdly troubled. He shook his head. "I just think you should make your own music the way you want to do it. Not let others do it for you."

Kate held up a hand. "Wait—"

She wanted to listen because they were playing her song again. But this time through the monitors came a lush sonic landscape of beats, loops, and synths. There was no trace of Lucinda. There was her voice, coming in above the heavy instrumentation, sounding the same and yet utterly different. Bigger. Better. Brighter.

"Wow," she said.

"This is crazy," Drew said quietly. "You're not going to sound like this at the showcase."

Kate turned to him. "So what? They'll see what I can do by myself—and then they'll listen to this and see what I can do with a little help."

"A *little* help?" Drew repeated. "Is that how you'd describe totally changing everything about your music? You can't just switch up your sound like you can switch up your hair color."

"I thought you liked my hair!"

Drew sighed. "It's great, but that's not what I'm talking about. I'm talking about how there aren't even any real *instruments* in the song now."

"So?"

"So it's not you, Kate. It's you selling out."

"*Selling out?*" She couldn't believe he'd used that term. It infuriated her. "Oh, okay, Mr. Integrity. Maybe that should be your new tattoo. I think there's a tiny bare spot on your right arm."

Drew stared at her in disbelief.

She felt a momentary flutter of guilt, but she was too mad to stop now. He'd been acting weird this whole time, and she didn't like it one bit. "And if that's how you feel about it, maybe you should go."

Drew stood up. "Okay," he said. "I will." He turned to go, then came back and gave her a quick kiss on the top of her head. It didn't feel sweet or romantic, though. It felt like a big bug had landed on her hair, and then flown off.

Kate stayed on the couch, fuming. What right did he have to question her manager and these producers? He was a college student. An *intern*.

The Kate she was hearing now over the monitors? She didn't sound like a girl who used to nearly pass out from stage fright. She didn't sound like a girl from small-town Ohio. She didn't sound like the Boring One. No, she sounded like a *star*.

The only people who bitch about sellouts, she thought, *are the people no one wants to buy.*

By the time she left, late that evening, she had demos of three songs that Todd promised to share with the A&R execs at her showcase. They sounded incredible. Not very much like the songs as she'd written them to be—but still incredible.

When she pulled into the lot of Park Towers, she was still trying to decide how mad she was at Drew. Was he looking out for her best interests, or trying to cramp her style? Maybe he didn't want her to succeed because he was afraid she'd leave him behind.

17

A LITTLE RED CARPET THING

Madison gave a low whistle when she saw the post on *D-Lish*. *Wow,* she thought, *that sucks for everyone.* (But it was also sort of amusing, because who didn't love romantic gossip?)

The accompanying picture was a blurry cell phone shot, but the article was damning enough:

> Looks like things are getting nasty on the set of *The Fame Game*. Starlet Carmen Curtis, supposed BFF of indie-pop cutie Kate Hayes, is either a *really* bad friend or was only playing nice on TV. She *is* an actress after all! Well, the sometime-sweetheart of Aussie heartthrob Luke Kelly (who's currently overseas filming) apparently couldn't keep her hands to herself last weekend. At a scenester party in Silver Lake, she got caught making out with Kate's boyfriend. Carmen, we thought you already had your Romeo, girl! Why are you pawing someone else's?!! Foul play!

Madison reached for her phone and dialed Kate. She wasn't surprised that there was no answer. "Hey," she said to her voice mail, "I just saw *D-Lish*. I hope it's not true. Is it? Did you know? Should we start planning Mission Take Down Carmen? Call me."

"Hope what's not true?" Gaby asked, wandering into the living room with one of her trademark smoothies in hand.

Wordlessly, Madison flipped her computer screen around. Gaby leaned over, her lips moving as she read the news.

"Yikes," she said when she was done. "That's the party we were at. The one where they served all those shish kebab things? Kate dropped one on her lap." She giggled. "Then Jay picked it up off her skirt and ate it."

"I totally did not need to know that," Madison said.

She skimmed the article again. It *had* to be true. The writers at *D-Lish* usually used blind items when they couldn't confirm their intel. This, Madison assumed, was a reaction to a lawsuit filed by a former *Top Act* host. *D-Lish* had accused him of having an affair after being photographed hugging a much younger woman, who ended up being his seventeen-year-old niece.

Madison wondered why Kate hadn't called her to talk about it—surely Drew, aka Mr. Nice Guy, had told her immediately after it happened. Hadn't Madison proved herself a good confidante? A trusted friend? (Even if she'd gotten Kate in a *teensy* bit of trouble for the drastic haircut.)

If Kate had called her, Madison could have offered helpful advice. She would have told her to lay low for a few days; would have assured her that people would stop talking about it as soon as anyone else misbehaved, which would be any second now; would have explained that *everyone* kissed *everyone* in Hollywood, especially at parties. Madison personally knew a few starlets for whom hooking up with randoms was about as consistent as their gym routines.

Madison almost found herself feeling a bit sorry for Carmen, too. No, the two of them had never really gotten along, but Madison imagined that Carmen was feeling pretty ashamed of herself. She'd probably had too much to drink, and she'd had a moment of possessiveness. Drew had been hers first, after all. And, without thinking, she'd tried to restake her old claim on that tattooed giant. (Madison never saw Drew's appeal, but to each her own.)

Since Madison had an affair or two under her Prada belt, she knew not to cast the first stone. But she didn't excuse Carmen for her actions. Especially considering the fraught boy history Carmen already had with Kate. The world didn't know that Kate had dated Luke first, but Madison did. So kissing Drew made Carmen seem like just another rich Daddy's girl, one who assumed she could have whatever she wanted, and who didn't stop to think about the consequences of her actions.

As someone who was living daily with the consequences of her actions—or, more accurately, *Charlie's* actions—Madison resented such a casual attitude.

There were definitely some awkward silences going on down in her old apartment, provided Carmen hadn't tucked her tail between her legs and run back to Topanga into the arms of Mommy and Daddy Curtis.

Madison shut her laptop and resolved to push all thoughts of the situation from her mind. Publicity was publicity, after all, and most people in L.A. would kill for it. (Which was why, the moment a would-be actress saw her star dimming, the world would "discover" a "stolen" sex tape. As if people couldn't figure out the desperate truth. Madison had vowed *never* to be in that position. No pun intended.)

"You want to go down to the pool?" Gaby asked.

"I would," Madison said, "but I've got to get ready. There's a little red carpet thing." She saw Gaby's eyes widen, and a hurt expression crossed her face. "Emphasis on 'little,'" she added. "Trust me, you're not missing anything."

"Okay . . . ," Gaby said uncertainly.

Madison blew her a kiss, then walked into her room and over to her spacious closet, with its bright, beautiful clothes hung in neat rows. She selected a scarlet dress by Alice + Olivia that ShopAddict, the designer publicity firm, had sent over the week before. Madison couldn't help it; she liked to wear red on the red carpet. She was never one to blend in with her surroundings, but the color looked too good on her to resist.

This evening she was heading to a dinner for social

networking bigwigs. She hadn't been lying to Gaby—the event didn't sound amazing at all. But there would be a big media presence, insuring at least a handful of MADISON STUNS IN ALICE + OLIVIA headlines. Also, more importantly, she'd heard that an up-and-coming TV producer would be in attendance. He was quickly climbing the ranks over at the Gallery Network, PopTV's main competitor, and Madison had certain . . . *projects* she wanted to discuss with him. Beautyland, Madison's production company, had been on the back burner for months now, and it was time to start thinking about bringing it up to the front. Time to start focusing on #1: Herself.

Since Madison wasn't going to be running into Andrew Garfield or Liam Hemsworth at the event, she hadn't done her usual two-and-a-half-hour pre-carpet routine. (Facebook's Mark Zuckerberg was the guest of honor, and while he was cute in a sort of nerdy way, he was married.) But Madison had avoided salt and had drunk *gallons* of water in the past few days, so the size zero dress fit her perfectly. She'd gotten her hair blown out earlier in the day, and as for the makeup—she could take care of herself. The Glam squad was good for show, but truth be told, no one knew how to do a sultry eye and a nude lip better than Madison Parker.

As she dusted bronzer across her shoulders and décolletage, she heard Gaby turn on loud salsa music in the living room. Her roommate was probably going to spend the next three hours practicing for the *Dancing with the*

Stars audition that she insisted Trevor was lining up for her. She'd been doing that a lot lately. She'd been talking about setting up a barre in the living room, too, so she could practice her *ronde de jambes*, whatever *that* was.

Madison didn't mind salsa, per se, but suddenly dinner with internet geeks seemed a lot more appealing.

The carpet stretched a dozen yards from the sidewalk to the entrance of the Beverly Hills Cultural Center. Madison was slightly disappointed it wasn't longer, and for a moment she wondered if—salsa avoidance aside—it had been a mistake to come. But since she was only a few weeks past her days of scrubbing out dog cages in an oversized pair of Wellies, maybe she should look on the bright side.

She walked slowly toward the doors, stopping every few steps to pose for the photographers.

There were plenty of them at the event, and they *all* wanted her picture. An older couple had climbed out of their limo at the same time as Madison, and the paparazzi yelled at them to get out of the shot. The couple were probably billionaire investors in the next big social media venture, but they were in their sixties and unphotogenic, so the paparazzi wanted nothing to do with them—and *everything* to do with Madison.

She was standing with one hand on a cocked hip, a mysterious closed-lip smile on her face, when she spotted a familiar face in the crowd. Ryan Tucker.

What in the world was he doing here? It took all of

Madison's cool to not go sprinting toward him. She made herself keep posing while she counted to ten—a respectable delay in her reaction, she thought. She'd gotten to number six when she realized what she should have known right away: It was not Ryan Tucker at all. As the figure moved closer, he came into better focus; he was just another handsome Hollywood type with sun-lightened hair and a chiseled jaw.

Madison fought her disappointment with a brilliant smile. She decided to sign some autographs, too, and then she posed for a picture with a teenage girl who looked like she might jump out of her skin with excitement. (It never hurt to be photographed interacting with fans. It was good for her image, and so much easier than responding to their fan mail like Kate.)

Forget Ryan Tucker. *This* was what life was supposed to be like, she thought. Flashbulbs. Fans. Adoration. Now if only Nick would line up some of the mega-endorsement deals he'd been talking about, she'd be back in business.

Or: if her conversation went well with Jack Stanbro, a Gallery executive.

She needed to find Jack before the dinner began. Because if there were awards—and there were *always* awards at these things—people tended to duck out for a smoke or a cell phone call and never return.

She'd never met Jack, but she'd Google-imaged him, so she knew what to look for: a thirty-something man with hipster glasses, hair cropped close to his head, and a mole on his right cheek. In pictures, he was better than average looking, but Madison knew not to rely on publicity shots for *that* kind of information. She'd seen plenty of shots of Trevor Lord that made him look like a *GQ* model.

After fifteen minutes of searching, Madison spotted Jack over by the bar. She swiped a glass of Champagne from a passing waiter and made her approach. He was typing into his iPhone and frowning in concentration. Madison waited as patiently as she possibly could—for five seconds—and then said, "Excuse me, aren't you Jack Stanbro?"

He looked up, startled. He wasn't so powerful yet that he expected to be recognized. "Guilty as charged. And whom do I have—" Then he stopped himself. And smiled at her. "*I* know you. You're the infamous Madison Parker."

"Guilty as charged," Madison repeated, smiling back. "Not to steal your line."

Jack laughed. "I'm pretty sure I wasn't the one to coin it." Up close, he was at least as handsome as his pictures, if not more. (Again, *why* was it that she couldn't go on dates with guys who had actual *jobs*?)

"So I've been reading some pretty interesting things about you lately," Madison said, leaning an elbow on the bar.

Jack raised his eyebrows. "In the trade magazines?"

"Of course. You don't think I only read tabloids and women's magazines, do you? I keep up on things, Jack. I like to know what's going on in the industry. I own a production company, after all." She took a delicate sip of Champagne. "I happen to know that you're looking to develop some new unscripted shows, and I think we might have some ideas to talk about."

Jack's eyebrows lifted even higher. "Oh really," he said. "I'm surprised you aren't talking to PopTV about this. You've done two huge shows with them."

"Actually, three if you include my self-produced make-over show," she reminded him. "But I'm a planner." She took a step closer. "I always like to know my next move. And I've got some big ideas that I thought you might want to hear." She gave her hair a subtle toss. "I love the cameras, Jack, but not only being in front of them. I'm really eager to get into development."

Jack nodded. "This is all very interesting, Madison," he said. "I'm not sure that now is the time"—he gestured to the event going on around them—"but I'd definitely like to hear whatever you have on your mind."

"Shall we set a date, then?" She lingered on the word "date," just in case. There wasn't a wedding ring on his finger, after all, and unlike Ryan, Jack wasn't allergic to the camera. Though the thought of going on a *real* date with anyone right now didn't actually appeal to Madison, she thought it made good business sense to keep her options open.

Jack brought out a silver card case. "Let's," he said, pulling a card out and handing it to Madison. "Here's my info. Set it up with my assistant."

Madison agreed to call in the morning and said a polite good-bye. When she shook his hand and made her way to her table, she did so feeling about nine feet tall. She wasn't always going to be Trevor's pawn. No way. Someday soon she was going to be a queen.

18

A SHORT COMMUNICATION BREAK

Carmen slammed her car door and dashed up the steps to Siren Studios on Sunset. She was half an hour late to the full-cast photo shoot. Laurel was going to be furious, and Carmen's excuse wasn't going to cut it.

She pulled open the door, already imagining Laurel's stressed, over-caffeinated voice. *Oh, sure, no problem! You're late because you had to come all the way from Topanga, because you pissed off your roommate so much that you had to spend the night at your parents'. No big deal! And then Luke told you that maybe his pal Eric should watch his plants, since you were so busy kissing other guys. Sure, Carmen, I get it! Great! Come on in and get your hair and makeup done, sweetheart!*

She hurried toward the studio at the back of the warehouse, praying that someone else—Gaby, maybe—was even later than she was.

The shoot was for the May cover of *Seventeen* magazine, so the giant, high-ceilinged room had been filled with flowers, potted trees, a picnic table, and fake birds.

If something was even vaguely springy, the prop guys had brought it. (There was even a wheelbarrow—what were they supposed to do with *that*?) The air smelled like a florist's shop, and also like dirt.

Laurel came right up to Carmen, her expression dark.

"I'm so sorry—" Carmen began.

Laurel held up a hand. "Let's just get going, shall we? Follow me, you're down this way." She led Carmen to a small windowless room in which a makeup girl sat, thumbing through *Vogue*. "Have a seat," Laurel said. "We shoot in an hour."

She was already leaving when Carmen called after her. "Where's everyone else?" Carmen had the stupid, momentary hope that she, in fact, was the *first* one to arrive.

Laurel paused for a moment. "They're getting ready, too . . . in a different room."

Carmen drew back in surprise. "What do you mean?"

"I mean that Kate would rather not be around you at the moment, and we only have two dressing rooms to work with. So they're in one, and you're in the other. I'm sorry, but it's the only way we could get Kate to agree to show up today."

Carmen's jaw dropped. "*Really?* You're putting me in solitary?"

Laurel sighed. "Don't overreact, Carmen. You're getting your makeup done."

"Fine, I'm being quarantined then."

"Would you rather we put Kate by herself? She's what

most would consider the wronged party here."

"I didn't wrong her," Carmen nearly yelled. "I made a mistake, a tiny mistake, and I don't know why everyone has to act like it's the end of the world!"

When Laurel didn't reply, Carmen flopped down into the makeup chair. "Make me look slutty," she told the girl. "Since that's the message I'm getting from my producer here."

The girl looked toward Laurel, who shook her head grimly. "Make her look like she's not totally overreacting," she said. "Peachy cheeks, false eyelashes—but not a lot of eye shadow—and a warm, glossy lip. I'll have them send in some of the inspiration photos they're working off of."

Carmen rolled her eyes. "Laurel," she said. "We talked about this. I told you what happened. How it wasn't anything—"

"I know," Laurel said, her voice gentler now. "And honestly, I don't think it's as big of a deal as everyone is making it, except in that it makes my job a lot more difficult today. But *Kate* seems to think it's a big deal, and since she is a bit more fragile than you, she's getting some extra attention." She gave Carmen a tired smile, then hurried down the hall.

Carmen let out a frustrated sigh. It was all such a stupid, stupid mistake—why did the whole world have to know about it?

Because she left her mike pack on, that's why. But it *wasn't* Trevor or Laurel who'd talked to the press. They hated it when the tabloids broke stories they could have broken on the show; *they* wanted that privilege. Sure, a blind item or a teaser never hurt, but giving away the entire story line didn't do much for their ratings.

The party had been packed, so in a way, it could have been anyone. But Carmen was certain it was Lily. And unlike the lie about Carmen's roving eye, Carmen had no plausible deniability for the kiss. She was mad at everyone today—including herself.

The question was, why was Lily doing this to her? She'd thought they were *friends*.

"Okay, I want Gaby over there by the fern with the pruning shears. Madison, you sit in the deck chair with the bottle of tanning oil. Kate, you'll have the pitcher of lemonade and be pouring it for Carmen, who'll be here at the picnic table."

Kate muttered something, and the photographer, who'd been the one giving the directions, said, "Excuse me?"

"I'm not pouring her a drink," Kate said, louder this time.

"Ummm . . . okay. Do you have a problem with the creative direction or . . . ?"

Kate walked over to Gaby and took the shears away. "I'll be the gardener and Gaby can deal with . . . *her*."

Carmen opened her mouth to offer a snide retort, but then thought better of it. No sense in pissing off Laurel even more by getting into a fight with her costar, even though Kate—who looked like freaking Tinkerbell in that lime-green mini and those weird ankle boots—was acting insane.

She glanced down at her own dress, a gauzy, persimmon-colored stunner by Marchesa. She might have gotten a bum deal on the dressing room, but she definitely had the best dress.

"I can pour," Carmen said. "I can play waitress." *Though Kate's the one with the experience in that arena*, she thought.

Laurel whispered something to the photographer, whose eyes flicked between them with cold appraisal.

"Let's have Kate and Madison side by side," he said. "Gaby and Carmen can take turns playing hostess. Can someone please move that bluebird? And that idiotic wheelbarrow? Let's not have this look like a set from *Sesame Street*, all right?"

The "story" for the shoot was that the girls were throwing a garden party. Ideally, they ought to be laughing and talking together while being photographed, which would give the fanciful, purposely artificial set an air of real fun, real *life*. But Kate would hardly acknowledge Carmen's existence. Madison seemed normal enough— she was *never* the picture of warmth to Carmen—but Gaby had that glassy look Carmen remembered all too well. Was it possible she was taking pills again? Had she spiked her lunchtime smoothie with a couple shots of Patrón?

"Gab," she whispered when they were switching spots, "are you okay?" Carmen handed her the pitcher and got ready to position herself at the picnic table, which was set with bright, cheerful place settings, complete with fake salads and a baguette that looked like it had been shellacked.

Gaby smiled hazily and nodded. Then she stumbled in her heels and dropped the pitcher on the floor, splashing water all over her dress.

"Wardrobe! We need you on set," yelled the photographer.

"Okay, we need a costume change or a hair dryer," Laurel said, appearing at Gaby's elbow and steering her back toward the dressing room. "We'll be quick," she said to the room at large.

Madison and Kate began whispering to each other. Carmen, feeling angry and left out, wished she had her iPhone to pull out. At least then she could scroll through email rather than sit here like the reject in the high school cafeteria.

She stood up. "I'm going to—"

"Please sit back down," the photographer said. "I'm reframing. And reconsidering."

Reconsidering what? Carmen wondered. Taking the job of photographing such rank amateurs in the first place? Because that's what they were acting like—you'd think they'd never been at a photo shoot before, when in fact it was probably their fiftieth.

It took everything in Carmen not to lose her cool, but

she knew better. On a cover shoot, the writer who was doing the accompanying article was almost always present. An on-set blowup would overshadow anything positive the magazine would have to say about her blossoming career. And CARMEN CURTIS THROWS PHOTO-SHOOT HISSY FIT was not a headline she was interested in reading. She'd had enough bad press lately.

She picked idly at a potted hydrangea bush and tried not to wonder if Kate and Madison were talking about her. Carmen had attempted to talk to Kate about the kiss, but Kate had made it very clear she wasn't interested in explanations. Drew, too, was ignoring her. First she couldn't breathe without the two of them in her face. Now they were both avoiding her like the plague. After failing to respond to about five million of her texts, he'd finally written to say that he was really busy with work and school, and maybe they should take a short communication break.

That had hurt—even more than knowing that she had, in a moment of drunken stupidity, betrayed her friend and roommate. She and Drew had *never* taken a "communication break." Sure, there were times when they talked less often—like when she was filming *The End of Love* eighteen hours a day—but she always knew Drew was out there, only a phone call or a text message away. She had counted on that, and she hadn't even known how much.

"Okay, let's get this thing started up again," Laurel said, escorting Gaby to her place.

Gaby's new dress was yellow, with eyelet trim. It was

sweet and innocent-looking, which Carmen supposed Gaby had been, too, before Hollywood got its hands on her.

"Sorry," Gaby whispered.

Carmen shrugged. "No worries," she said. "You want me to pour?"

Gaby nodded. "That's probably best."

The rest of the shoot was uneventful, if uncomfortable. Carmen hoped their smiles would look genuine. And if they didn't, that there was someone on the *Seventeen* staff who was really good at Photoshop, and could give them the aura of warmth they lacked.

When they finally broke for the day, Carmen ducked her head and hurried to find her clothes. She prayed that Laurel wouldn't follow her to berate her some more, and thankfully, she didn't.

Carmen felt her spirits lift a little as she exited the building. She was relieved to be back in her worn-in, beloved Rag & Bone jeans and out of that airless studio. She might have felt almost happy, had she not stumbled into a small crowd of fans who were waiting in the parking lot. And unfortunately, they were not alone. In addition to the people grasping small stacks of glossy prints, Sharpies, and digital cameras, there were several paparazzi, one of whom held a video camera.

"Oh. It's just Carmen," someone said, sounding disappointed. "Where's Madison?"

"Boyfriend stealer," someone else yelled.

Carmen felt a pang of embarrassment. It was one thing to be insulted by a stranger; it was another to have it filmed. Who were these people, and why were they yelling at her? How had they known she was here?

She turned around to look at the building and saw Madison Parker make her exit, already waving adoringly to the crowd. Carmen gritted her teeth. Obviously @missmadparker had tweeted her location in one of her fantastically self-serving tweets. *Photo shoot with the girls at Siren Studios! Can you say glamour???!!!! XOXO.*

Carmen could have strangled her. But she wouldn't—of course. For one thing, she wasn't into violence, and for another, the last thing she needed right now was another enemy.

19

DON'T WORRY, BABE,
I STILL LIKE YOU

Kate couldn't believe the mess her life had become. Less than two weeks before her showcase, which was basically the most important day of her life, her roommate and her boyfriend decide to make out at the house party of some Silver Lake heiress. And apparently they'd done it without caring who was looking; whereas some people knew how to keep their indiscretions hidden, others were seemingly too drunk to bother. It was infuriating; it was humiliating; it was *everything that she did not want to deal with right now.*

Kate didn't want to process it. She didn't want to think about it or talk about it. She wanted it Never to Have Happened.

But it had, of course, and now it was a Thursday evening that she normally would have spent with Lucinda, and instead she had to film a pickup scene with Carmen "I Kiss Other People's Boyfriends" Curtis.

Laurel had arrived early to make sure Kate was

wearing the correct outfit for the scene. She rattled off pieces she had noted in her notebook, expecting Kate to find them amidst the general mess of her closet. It was an annoying new Trevor-enforced policy, and they had to do it every time they shot a pickup scene. Everything from their clothes to their nail polish color was documented, and the girls were instructed to throw out nothing. That way, when they needed a scene to take place directly after one that had already been shot (meaning, according to TV time, they wouldn't have had the opportunity to change their clothes, hair, or nails), they could easily replicate the look. Now Kate was sitting on the living room couch, in an outfit that frankly looked a little rumpled, emotionally preparing herself to play nice.

"Are you sure that's the same polish you had on before?" Laurel called from the kitchen.

"I mean, it's red. Do you really think anyone is going to be able to tell the difference?" Kate responded, examining her ruby nails.

"Trevor will notice, and I'll be the one to face his wrath if we have to color correct. It's expensive and takes forever."

"It'll be fine," Kate assured her.

To add insult to injury, Kate was not only going to have to smile through this scene acting like Carmen hadn't just pulled the ultimate girl betrayal, she was going to have to do it in a *wig*. A good wig, yes—one that looked remarkably like her former strawberry-blond waves—but still. Someone else's dead hair. It was sitting there on the coffee table, waiting for her to put it on. She nudged it with her foot and scowled.

Her apartment felt cold and empty, even with Laurel and the crew shuffling around her setting up, and the security guy sitting in the corner, playing Angry Birds on his iPhone. Carmen had been staying at her parents' house, and Drew had booked a quick and conveniently timed trip to New York with a couple of other Rock It! interns.

Kate wasn't mad at him anymore, and in fact she missed him, though it'd only been twelve hours since they last saw each other. Of course she'd been furious at first, though Drew swore up and down that the kiss was nothing and that he'd stopped it immediately.

"That's what they all say," Madison had noted when Kate told her. "Does a man ever say, 'Oh yeah, I kissed someone else and it was totally awesome. But don't worry, babe, I still like you'? Drew's a good guy, I know. But still. You should ask Laurel. She'll know what happened."

Kate still couldn't believe the kiss had been caught on audio. She had to wonder what would have happened if no one at the party had seen it. If it hadn't gotten leaked to D-Lish, would Trevor have wanted to use the audio on the show? Would he have engineered a terrible surprise for Kate—say, somehow have her find out about it on camera?

Kate was glad that Trevor hadn't been given that option. Because she realized that the situation could have been even worse than it was.

When Kate asked Laurel what she knew about the kiss, Laurel had assured her that it really was one-sided. And considering that it was basically an unwritten part of Laurel's job to stir up drama, Kate realized she had no reason to lie. "Drew was, like, 'What do you think you're doing?'" Laurel told her. "You don't have to worry about him."

But Kate *had* worried. She couldn't help thinking about how Carmen and Drew had known each other for so many years. Their friendship was deep and probably complicated, as most old relationships tended to be. (Look how long it had taken her to free herself from Ethan the underminer!) Compared to Carmen, Kate was the new kid on the block, and she didn't like feeling that way at all. Which was why she'd finally made Laurel play her the audio from the Silver Lake party.

Her heart pounded as she listened. Through the speakers in the PopTV editing bay, she could hear the thudding bass from the party host's top-of-the-line stereo system. Then came Carmen's voice, full of laughter, and Drew's deeper tones. They were reminiscing about some awesome experience they'd shared back in high school, something about the beach and hot cocoa, and Carmen sounded like she might simply *melt* from the wonderful Norman Rockwell nostalgia. Kate gritted her teeth. (And all the while Kate had been outside by the pool, obliviously eating shish kebabs with Gaby and Jay!)

Then she glanced over at Laurel. "Now," Laurel had whispered.

First there was silence, broken only by the background music—Rihanna singing *"Like an actor on a movie screen / You played the part with every line."*

Kate stiffened, knowing what the silence on the tape meant. *Carmen is kissing Drew right now*, she thought. *I can't believe I'm hearing it.*

But then came the moment she'd been waiting for. Drew's voice, shocked. "Whoa, Carmen," she heard him say. "What are you doing?" Pause. "You *kissed* me."

Laurel had clicked off the sound. "See?" she'd said. "I told you."

Laurel made Kate swear that she'd never tell anyone that she had played her the tape. It had made Kate feel better, definitely. But she'd had to have a minor fight with Drew anyway, because he'd waited a full twenty-four hours before telling her.

At dinner she'd confronted him. "You sat there next to me in the studio, knowing that *the night before* you'd kissed my roommate, and you didn't say anything to me? Is that why you were acting so weird that day? Your *guilty conscience*?" she'd demanded.

Drew hunched his shoulders. "I didn't want Carmen to kiss me. I didn't *ask* her to kiss me. I didn't do anything wrong, Kate."

"But you should have told me," she insisted.

"And have you get all upset when you were supposed to be focusing on your career? I was trying to do the right thing. I didn't want to distract you."

Kate understood that this made sense. But she was still upset. "You and Carmen have known each other forever. She's had plenty of time to make out with you before now. So why is she doing it when you're my boyfriend? Why does she try to take everything away from me?"

Drew had reached out and taken her hand. "She's not, Kate. She's not trying to do anything like that."

"Don't defend her," Kate snapped.

"She was drunk and, I don't know, feeling lonely. I'm her oldest friend, and I can't do anything about that. I wouldn't want to, anyway. She's a good person, Kate. She's just not very careful sometimes. You know that. Remember that she's your friend, too."

"Was," Kate said.

"Oh, Katie." Drew sighed. "Please don't make this into a bigger deal than it is. I am with you. Not Carmen."

Then he had pulled her toward him, and she found herself snuggling into his broad warm chest. It was almost against her will, but it felt so nice. "I guess I forgive you," she said eventually. "But next time you want to make out with someone? Tell me, okay?"

"Okay." He paused. "I want to make out with someone."

She started. "Wha—"

"You," he interrupted. And then he'd pressed his lips to hers.

Now here she was, having to go back in time for the cameras, having to pretend that none of it had happened.

"Carmen's on her way up," Laurel said. "Let's get this wig on you."

The lighting in the room was dimmer than the crew usually used, so when Kate looked in the mirror she saw a girl who looked exactly like old Kate. She touched the tips of the wig delicately, suddenly missing her real hair. The platinum pixie had been a hit with the press, and had even brought comparisons to Michelle Williams's cute 'do, but it left Kate with very few styling options.

When Carmen arrived, Laurel did a continuity check.

"I had to get this blouse emergency dry-cleaned," Carmen said, holding out a sleeve. "I got olive oil on it."

"Good job," Laurel said. Satisfied with her inspection, she led Carmen into the room.

Kate and Carmen didn't meet each other's eyes, but Kate heard her murmur a shy "Hey."

Laurel snapped her fingers. "Okay, ladies, so we're back to the part where you're talking about whether or not Sophia has feelings for Jay, and what that means for Gaby. This is our A story, so we need a scene with you guys reacting, talking about how Gaby is going to handle it now that she's sober."

If she's sober, Kate thought.

Laurel gave them a falsely cheerful smile. "Okay?" She looked down at her notes. "Also, if you could mention that Sophia invited Jay to lunch the other day that would be great." She leaned in a little closer and lowered her voice. "Look, I know neither one of you wants to be here, but we really need this scene to pull the episode together, so let's hit our points and we'll be done quickly."

"'Quickly' sounds good," Kate said coldly.

Laurel smiled uncomfortably at the two girls. "Right. Let's get the camera rolling, okay?"

And so Carmen and Kate sat in the living room together, pretending that it was two weeks ago and they weren't in a fight.

"Nice hair," Carmen said, smiling.

The compliment would end up on the cutting room floor, obviously, but it was an attempt at breaking the ice. A joke.

Well, Kate didn't think it was funny. She smiled back thinly. She was going to hit her lines and be done with this shoot as soon as humanly possible. "Did you hear that Sophia and Jay have been hanging out?"

Carmen nodded. "I know. I can't say I'm that surprised, but it's pretty uncool of them. Do you think that Gaby knows? I'd be kind of upset if my friend was calling the guy I was dating to hang out."

Kate realized the deep irony of this staged conversation, given her and Carmen's complicated romantic crossovers. They'd practically partner-swapped. She waited a beat or two, letting the camera capture her bemused expression as Madison had coached her. "Yeah. It's *really* uncool of Sophia," she said. "Just because she likes Jay, or thinks he's hot or whatever, it doesn't mean she can, like, *go* for him. Honestly, what kind of girl does that?"

Carmen tossed her head, sending her long, dark hair over her shoulder. "Sophia is a free spirit," she said. "I'm sure she means no harm."

Kate barked a laugh. "That girl is *not* harmless. God, ask her sister about that sometime."

"Well, maybe she wasn't really thinking about it that way," Carmen said, an edge creeping into her voice. "Maybe she and Jay are just good friends."

Kate understood that the conversation had shifted, and they were talking not about Sophia and Jay, but about Carmen and Drew. She leaned forward. "Maybe *Sophia* should learn that being a spoiled brat and thinking she should get whatever she wants is not an excuse for making a play for someone else's boyfriend."

"Well, maybe *Sophia* thinks *Gaby's* overreacting," Carmen replied.

From behind the cameras Laurel shouted, "Kate, take off the wig!"

Kate pulled the wig off and threw it out of frame before continuing. She instinctually tugged off her sweater, too, so she'd look different if they used clips from both conversations. Madison had taught her well. Trevor might get a pickup scene *and* a fight out of one single night's reel. "I realize that you're used to getting your way, Carmen. I know Mommy and Daddy gave you everything you ever wanted. But you can't have *everything*."

"Don't be—"

Kate didn't let her go on. "You can't steal someone's

boyfriend. Drew isn't a Phillip Lim tank top."

"You know I didn't steal that, Kate," Carmen said. Her cheeks were flushed. "And you know that Drew and I are like this"—she held up two crossed fingers—"and that we were best friends when you were still in Ohio, wearing your hair in pigtails and fantasizing about trying out for the cheerleading team."

Kate scoffed. "Don't make this about me," she said. "You're the one who did a terrible thing, and for the first time in your life, you're having to pay for your actions."

"Like you've never made a mistake? Because I seem to remember you stumbling through a live-air interview, so blitzed on Xanax that you could barely pronounce your own name."

Kate lowered her voice. She was seriously pissed now. "Like I said, *Little CC*, don't make this about me. It's about you. And Drew doesn't like you in that way, in case he didn't make that clear enough by turning you down. He likes me."

Carmen stood up. "I don't want to be having this conversation anymore," she said. Then she took off her mike pack, dropped it on the floor, and left, waving to Laurel on the way out. "I hope you got what you needed. I hope you're happy," she called, and slammed the door behind her.

Laurel came hurrying over. "Did I ever," she said to Kate. "That was great."

Kate wished she could share Laurel's enthusiasm. She

didn't want to fight over Drew anymore. She wanted the drama to be over, and she knew he did, too. A sinking feeling in her stomach told her that Drew wouldn't like being the subject of a fight—especially when that fight was going to be aired on national TV.

She sighed heavily. "I think I need to go for a walk. You're done with me for the night, right?"

Laurel nodded and waved her on—her phone was ringing. No doubt Trevor was calling to check up on the shoot. The security guy was still lost in his Angry Birds game and didn't even notice Kate slip by.

Kate went downstairs and stepped outside into the cool evening, but then she stopped in confusion. She didn't have a destination in mind, and she'd never just taken a *walk* from her place in Park Towers. She'd drive to Griffith Park or Runyon to hike, or else she'd drive to La Brea for a stroll and some window-shopping. What should she do now? Where should she go? L.A. felt strange and unfamiliar all of a sudden—as if she'd traveled back in time to the day she arrived, wide-eyed and nervous, toting Lucinda, a few boxes of books, and a wardrobe sourced almost exclusively from Old Navy.

Kate shook her head and pulled out her phone. Maybe she'd call Drew while dipping her toes in the Park Towers hot tub. He'd help her feel more at home (even if he was way off somewhere in the East Village). She was dialing him when she heard someone yelling her name, *Kate-HayesKateHayes*, like it was all one word. She looked up and saw a tall, slender, red-haired guy rushing toward her.

"KateHayes, I've written you so many letters, why haven't you written me back?" His voice was breathless and excited. He was grinning at her, but there was something wrong with this smile—he looked completely and totally insane.

"It's me, J.B.," he cried as he approached her. "I couldn't wait any longer to see you."

Kate gave her stalker one horrified glance, and then she turned and *sprinted* back inside.

20

PRETTY GOOD WHILE IT LASTED

Madison sat fidgeting in her seat at the small deli in Santa Monica. She'd already torn one cocktail napkin to shreds, and she was working on another. Was this a good idea? Or a terrible mistake?

Relax, she told herself. *It's not like there's an endorsement on the line here. Or a new show on Gallery.*

But as she watched Ryan Tucker enter the restaurant and walk across the room toward her, Madison realized that this lunch felt like a bigger deal than any business meeting. She offered him a small smile as he approached.

He leaned down and kissed her on the cheek. She flinched a little at his touch—not because she didn't want it, but because she did. More than she cared to admit.

A waiter started to approach them, but Madison waved him away. She wanted to have Ryan to herself, if only for a few more minutes.

Ryan might have had the same idea; he sat down across from her and pushed aside the menu without even looking at it. "You look beautiful," he said, his green eyes flashing. "How are you?"

He seemed glad to see her, but there was something guarded in his smile, Madison thought. It reminded her of the way he used to look at her, during her first weeks at Lost Paws. How sometimes he would stand in the hallway and watch her cleaning cages, shaking his head minutely, as if he were observing a person from a foreign place.

At the time, she'd found his behavior—and him—so annoying. She cleaned out cages like anyone else did; she just did so in better, trendier clothes. The irony of it hadn't been lost on her. Ryan had been born with a silver spoon in his mouth; Madison had come into the world with the equivalent of a plastic spork. Yet he'd taken her for a privileged brat.

Madison and Ryan came from radically different places, and they seemed to be heading in different directions, too. So what had brought them together? Sometimes Madison couldn't figure it out herself. They laughed at the same jokes; they shared a secret hatred of Pinkberry; they were both afraid of heights, deep water, and clowns. On the surface, it didn't seem like much. And yet they had a great time together. They understood each other. And they'd had a hard time keeping their hands off each other. All in all, it was pretty good while it lasted.

She felt a twinge of annoyance suddenly. It wasn't her fault everything had fallen apart. Maybe if Ryan hadn't gotten in that car accident that killed his best friend, being in the spotlight wouldn't have bothered him so much. She immediately felt bad for having such a thought.

"I'm good," she said belatedly. "Carmen and Kate are in a fight. Gaby might be drinking again. My sister is being her typical self, which means that I've been trying to avoid her as much as possible. And next week I'm meeting with a producer at a competing network to discuss my future in television. How about you?"

"Well, the shelter is expanding," Ryan said, the pride obvious in his voice. "We're building an addition on the back, which will house the so-called violent breeds—pits, rotts, mastiffs. . . ." He shook his head. "Everyone blames the pit bull, but do you know how vicious Chihuahuas can be? Those things don't care how small they are. They will *attack*."

"You think I don't remember Tiny? That guy nearly took a chunk out of my arm."

"Oh, riiiight," Ryan said, nodding. "I guess I forgot. Yeah, he's sorry about that."

"I might still have a scar." She held out her tanned, toned arm so he could inspect it. She knew perfectly well that there was no scar.

Ryan reached for her wrist and held it. "Looks good to me," he said. His fingers were warm and gentle on her skin.

Madison let herself enjoy the feeling for another moment before delicately pulling her arm away. "Do you want to order something?" she asked. She didn't even need to open the menu to know she wouldn't want anything; she'd never been a sandwich girl. Plus she'd told herself she'd start a cleanse this week, and today was as good a day as any to begin.

"I'll have a sandwich or something," he said.

"They have about fifty different kinds here," she pointed out.

He shrugged. "I'll tell them to surprise me."

Madison glanced around for the waiter, but instead met the eye of a woman at the table next to them. She nodded politely, and then turned back to Ryan. She'd seen the woman watching her in her peripheral vision.

"Recognized, huh?" Ryan asked. But it wasn't really a question.

"Pretty much always," she said. She kept her voice neutral, as if this were a simple fact as opposed to something she'd worked for every single day of her life. As if anonymity weren't a fate worse than death.

"I saw you the other day on the cover of *Life and Style*," he said.

She raised an eyebrow. "What were you doing reading *Life and Style*?"

"I was standing in line at the grocery store."

Madison smiled. She was well aware of the spread he was referring to, because she'd orchestrated it herself. She had called her favorite photographer and let him know that she and Kate Hayes would be hiking at Runyon. "Hiking helps her process her feelings of betrayal. I've really been a shoulder for her to lean on during this whole thing," Madison had said. She knew that this kind of information would help determine the caption, not to mention the photos that were selected.

And sure enough, it had. There were several shots of Kate looking thoughtful and sad, as well as shots of Madison looking attentive and sympathetic (in a sports bra). It was perfect, and Kate, who was learning the Way of Madison, was pleased with it. She was certainly defeating Carmen in the PR war. If the fight were actually about anything significant—which, when it came down to it, the kiss wasn't—Madison would have expected to see Team Kate and Team Carmen shirts lining windows of the crappy souvenir stores on Hollywood Boulevard.

But she didn't want to tell Ryan this. "You mean the shots of us hiking? Yeah, it's been sort of hard for Kate lately. I'm trying to be there for her."

Ryan reached out and touched Madison's wrist again. "You know, you don't have to do this. You don't have to create photo ops and hang out with people who're fighting over the same guy. You don't have to jump into a town car and hit a red carpet just because it's there."

"And what do you think I should do instead?" Madison asked, an edge coming into her voice. How had he known she'd staged the photos with Kate?

"You could come back to the shelter," Ryan said.

"Are you kidding? My *nails* finally grew back. I'm not going to do more manual labor."

"You could do PR stuff for us," he said.

"Is that why you wanted to have lunch? To ask me about coming to work for you?"

Ryan shook his head. "No. I wanted to see you. I'm saying all this to keep you here at the table with me."

"I wasn't leaving," Madison said.

"I know, but I keep thinking that you might."

"If you keep bossing me around," she said, "it gets more and more likely." But in truth, she kept having the urge to lean across the table and kiss him.

Not that she was going to.

"I want what's best for you," Ryan said. "I wish you hung out with . . . healthier people."

Madison bristled. Ryan was just trying to be nice, but it felt more like she was being judged. "Like you and your perfect family? Well, we don't all have happy J. Crew models for parents and adorable twin sisters. Some of us have had a harder life, Ryan, and we have to work to stay on top."

Ryan ran his hands through his hair. "Madison, I don't want to fight with you. I was trying . . . I don't know. I'm trying to make you understand that I care about you."

"But not enough to be with me."

He leaned forward. "It's not that. It's just that . . . I want to be a part of your life, but I can't be in *that* part of your life."

"Yeah, I've heard this stuff before," Madison said. "I can choose you or the camera."

"I didn't say that."

"But you did, Ryan, you only used more words to do it. So maybe you're fighting the good fight, saving animals, all that. Maybe you know something about a giant trust you're coming into the moment you hit twenty-five. Hooray. Maybe you feel settled. Well, good for you! But don't question my choices because they're different from the ones you'd make." She pushed her chair back from the table. The waiter, who had finally reappeared, stopped in his tracks. "I should probably get going," she said. Their relationship, *whatever* it was, was too complicated for her to deal with right now.

"But lunch—" Ryan began.

"I'm on a cleanse," Madison said. She stood. "It was really nice seeing you. And I mean that."

His eyes searched her face. "Mad, can't we talk some more?"

"I don't think so," she said softly. "Not right now." Then she turned and walked away.

She had a few thoughts to ponder as she waited for the valet to bring her Lexus around. One: She did want to see Ryan again, but she wasn't about to admit it to him. Two: She hoped he was smart enough to figure that out. Smart enough to try a bit harder to win her back. Three: It was *really* too bad that he wouldn't film, because that would have been a killer scene.

21

A STAR WAITING TO SHINE

"Of course, Mrs. Garcia," Trevor said, nodding sympathetically, though Mrs. Garcia couldn't see him through the phone. "We only want the best for your daughter. That's why we agreed to pay so much of her rehab costs, even though we, as a show and as a network, bear no responsibility for her use of alcohol or prescription drugs, or her subsequent . . . mishap." Trevor sounded calm, though he felt like throwing the phone across the room.

"It's not a healthy environment for Gabriela right now," Mrs. Garcia said. "She's a sensitive girl."

"She loves being on *The Fame Game*," Trevor pointed out. "I'm sure she told you that. Wasn't it her dream to come to Hollywood and pursue a career in the entertainment industry?"

He could hear Mr. Garcia murmuring something in the background, but Mrs. Garcia cut him off. "Fame is fleeting, Mr. Lord. But life is long. I want Gabriela to have a good life."

"Of course—every parent wants that," Trevor said. "But isn't it important what Gaby wants?" He bent a paper clip forward and back until it snapped.

"My daughter has not always acted in her own best interest," she said.

Tell me about it, Trevor thought. *Anyone could have told her that last round of implants was a terrible idea.*

"She is easily swayed. Easily taken advantage of," Mrs. Garcia went on.

"Let me assure you that no one associated with our show is taking advantage of her," Trevor said. "We're helping her. Honestly, things could have been a lot worse if we weren't around to keep an eye on her. And did she mention that we're about to get her on *Dancing with the Stars*? She's already booked a private coach to get ready before rehearsals begin." He made a mental note to have Laurel make this true, stat.

"We have spoken to a lawyer," Mrs. Garcia said.

Trevor winced. This was not news he wanted to hear. He whipped out his BlackBerry. GET ME LEGAL, he typed to Laurel.

"We are investigating—"

"Mrs. Garcia," Trevor interrupted. He knew that Gaby didn't want to leave the show, and since she was over eighteen, her parents couldn't simply take her away. But any time a lawyer was involved, things got ugly. "What if we agree on a probationary period? We'll watch Gaby very carefully, and you'll be in touch with her regularly, and if things ever seem less than perfect, we can discuss pulling her from the show." He took a sip of Evian. "Also, we can discuss a salary increase. . . ."

"Are you trying to bribe us?" Mrs. Garcia demanded.

"Not at all," said Trevor. "It seems to me like Gaby's had a bit of a rough time lately, and it might be a nice thing for her. Some extra spending money." He grimaced, grateful he wasn't having this conversation face-to-face.

After a moment, Mrs. Garcia sighed. "I'll talk with my daughter," she said. "We'll see."

A second after Trevor hung up the phone, Laurel hurried in. "They're at her house, you know," she said.

"Who? What?" Trevor asked.

"The Garcias. They called from her apartment."

Trevor put his head in his hands. Why was everyone such a headache lately? Sure, he'd talked the Garcias down—for now. And Laurel had gotten a few minutes of a Kate-Carmen fight, just as he'd hoped. And Madison was hitting every red carpet event he could get her an invite to, not to mention having comically bad dates with some of L.A.'s most ineligible bachelors. But nothing was ever as easy as it should be.

Trevor looked up at his producer. "Personality tests," he said. "Everyone's going to take them."

Laurel raised her eyebrows. "What? Why?"

"I need to make sure that Gaby's not the only loose

cannon around here. What if Kate regresses with her stage fright and then gets PTSD from a bad performance? Or what if her stalker shows up again? Nothing happened the other night, thank God—and no thanks to SoCal Security, who let her wander around alone at night. And what about that makeup girl Carmen said was spreading rumors about her? Not that she's ever on camera much, but still. I want all the main girls to meet with a psychologist. If anyone doesn't want to take a test, she can sign a waiver saying she won't sue us for emotional damages. We need to cover our asses."

"Wow," Laurel said. "Do you want me to take a test, too? Because sometimes I'm pretty sure this job is making me crazy."

Trevor's laugh was hollow. "I'm thinking about Sophia," he said. "Her parents aren't going to cause me any problems, but I'm ninety percent sure she might be a sociopath. See if you can make her sign the waiver. I don't even want to know what her results would say. She's about five different kinds of crazy."

Laurel nodded. "Seems possible, if not likely. Do you think it's true what they say, that she's sleeping with someone on the crew?"

Trevor shook his head. He had heard rumors but never a name. "Not the crew. She's a climber—she's not going to get it on with a PA. But . . ." He stopped. He felt like slapping himself on the forehead. How had he not thought of it before? He'd been seeing a *lot* more of her on the footage lately. And hadn't Stephen Marsh been pushing for her to get a better story line? Hadn't Stephen started talking about how Sophia was an underused character, a star waiting to shine?

He heaved a giant sigh. Stephen Marsh! She'd sunk her claws into him. The only question was: how far?

22

YOU GET ONE CHANCE

"So, how's the Next Big Thing doing this morning?" Kate's manager asked as he met her in the parking lot of SIR Los Angeles. Todd Barrows looked even happier and more upbeat than usual. "Ready for your big showcase?"

Kate fingered the latch on Lucinda's case. "I'm feeling good," she said. "Strong. Excited." She hoped that saying so would make it true. She was still feeling shaken by the appearance of J.B. On top of that, it felt like all her relationships were in an unpleasant state of flux. So it was kind of hard to focus on her music.

She knew she had to, though. This was everything she'd ever wanted. Everything she'd ever dreamed of, lying in her pink bedroom in Ohio. She'd worked for *years* for this. And it all came down to today. It was a lot of pressure, and as everyone who'd ever seen an episode of *The Fame Game* knew, Kate and Pressure didn't have the best track record.

"That's exactly what I want to hear, kiddo. Come along

this way," Todd said. "We've got the production stage all to ourselves." He yanked open the door and motioned for her to enter.

Kate sucked in her breath at what she saw before her. Although Todd had done his best to explain to her what a showcase looked like, she hadn't expected *this*. The room was huge: There was a stage on one end; a vast, empty floor in the middle; and a handful of couches scattered around in the back.

She could imagine how small she'd look onstage to the people sitting on those couches. There'd be no fans to cheer her on, no cluster of girls dancing, no one singing along to the chorus of "Love You Later."

Kate had thought she was afraid of big audiences, but suddenly she understood that having a small one was going to be a lot scarier.

She glanced down at her watch. Where was Drew? Even though he'd recently gotten back from New York and was swamped with work, he told her he'd be here. She was counting on being able to look up from her playing to catch his eye. She'd come to depend on the confidence boost he gave her.

"So you'll be up there, obviously," Todd said, pointing to the large stage, as if she might have somehow missed it, "and the studio execs will be back here." He gestured to the nearest couch.

"Do I really need all this . . . room?" she asked faintly. She remembered the claustrophobic sound booth she'd recorded "Starstruck" in with a pang of nostalgia. It had felt so small, so *safe*.

Todd nodded and gave her arm a friendly squeeze. "They want to see you onstage. It's not only how you sing, Kate. It's how you act when you're up there. You've got the voice of an angel—we know that. But do you have star power? Do you have charisma? Can you light up a room?"

She sank into a couch. Those weren't questions she wanted someone to ask her, not when she was fresh off being called Doormat all over *D-Lish*. (Although ever since she'd started taking Madison's advice, comments like that had gotten a lot less frequent.)

"Of course you do," Todd said, answering his own question. "That's why we're doing this. You've got something to prove, and today you're going to prove it."

He opened a leather binder and scanned down a page. "Fusion Music is first, then Dragonfly. Then we've got a break, then Merlin and GSA and Rogue Records. . . ."

Kate leaned down and took Lucinda out of the case. Her guitar, which she'd had since she was a *kid*, looked worse for the wear. She wished, for a moment, that she'd brought the shiny new electric one that *The Fame Game* had paid for. But she wasn't as confident on an electric guitar, and her demo would show the executives what she could do with some electronic and technological help . . . right?

A sound guy wandered in, chewing gum. "You ready to set up?" he asked.

Kate nodded and followed him onto the stage.

"Don't look so nervous, doll," Todd called. "You're going to be amazing. Oh, and if you're hungry? I ordered hors d'oeuvres."

"Awesome," Kate said. "Because when I'm about to have a panic attack, all I really want is a mini-bagel."

Todd held one out to her.

"I was kidding," she said, forcing a laugh.

Kate had been sitting onstage, her guitar in her lap, for what seemed like ages before the first group from Fusion Music filed in. Todd made a brief but gushing introduction as the four executives (all men) helped themselves to the snacks that had been laid out and checked their phones one last time before settling in for a listen.

Kate gave one final desperate look at the door. Where was Drew? Was he going to be a no-show? Her heart was racing even worse than it usually did, and he was always the one to calm her down. She wished she could check her phone for a message, but it was on the other side of the room.

Todd cleared his throat, and Kate knew she had to begin, with or without Drew. She leaned into the mike. "Hi, I'm Kate Hayes," she said, offering what she hoped was a confident smile. Then she felt like kicking herself, because of course they already knew that. "Thank you for coming," she added. "I appreciate your time. And I hope . . . I hope you like the show."

She took a deep breath and began to play. She'd decided

to start out with a new song, because she wanted to surprise them. "*I've been pacing this old room all night / thinking about our final fight / wishing I could say just what I meant. / But words are hard just like your eyes / I'm so tired of all your lies / the energy I had has all been spent. . . .*"

"Over You" was supposed to be her power song, the one aimed at all the sad, mad teenage girls in the world. (Because what teenage girl *wasn't* sad or mad at some point during the average day? Kate certainly was.)

In the second verse, the girl in the song realizes she has to stand up to her boyfriend, who then basically comes crawling back to her. It had seemed like such a good idea! It played to a market Kate knew she already appealed to.

But she could feel how the energy in the room had dampened. They didn't like the song. Did they think it was too bitter? It was supposed to be badass—like Christina Aguilera's "Fighter." Kate had written it to be spirited and catchy. But maybe that wasn't how it sounded to a bunch of middle-aged men. As she saw the first executive bring out his phone and begin tapping on it, her voice grew quieter and her playing became hesitant, and it was all she could do to finish the song she'd begun.

The next three songs went better, but far from great. And great, she knew, was what she needed to be.

Todd tried to reassure Kate after her set, when the Fusion Music people had shaken her hand and quickly vanished. "You were wonderful," he said. "You were."

"They hated me."

"They didn't. But maybe 'Over You' isn't the best opener. How about something a little more . . . positive?"

Kate nodded. She placed her hand over her pounding heart, willing it to calm down. She'd made a mistake in picking her first song, she could admit that. But it didn't have to affect everything. She could still pull this one out.

"You should feel confident," Todd urged her. "Do not feel pressure. Pressure is for when you have to do something you aren't prepared to do. But you are prepared for this. Now let's kick some butt, all right?"

"You sound like my sister. Or her basketball coach," Kate said.

Todd smiled. "Everybody wants to succeed. But the great musicians *expect* to succeed, and that includes you."

"You're still doing it," she said.

He shrugged. "What can I say? Get up there onstage and score a three-pointer."

But Kate's second set, for Dragonfly, went even worse. She dropped her pick, flubbed the bridge on "Love You Later," and by the time she finished her fourth song, she was on the verge of tears.

Todd, doing his best to hide his own shock, tried to do damage control. He told the A&R folks how brilliant Kate's recordings were. "She's having a rough day," he said. "Her grandpa died. Here, have a mini-bagel."

The executives nodded sympathetically but left looking grim, as if their attendance had been a colossal waste of time.

Which it was, Kate thought, feeling the tears come for real now. She'd done a terrible job. Everything was riding on today, and she was blowing it. *Where in the hell was Drew?*

After Todd closed the door behind the Dragonfly group, he turned to her, his face dark. "I have a feeling that another pep talk isn't going to do it for you today," he said.

Kate wiped her cheeks and said nothing. The tears kept coming.

"So—I think we should cancel the rest of the showcase."

If it was possible to feel relief and horror at the same time, Kate felt it now. "But—"

"I'm sorry," Todd said, his voice taking on an edge. "You get one chance with these people, Kate. I'm not going to risk you blowing the next three sets."

She sank down onto one of the couches, which sighed beneath her weight. How had she failed so badly? It was one thing to screw up an open mic, but a showcase? That was a whole other level of train wreck.

She wished she had a time machine. She needed a do-over.

She also wanted to crawl into her bed at home and have her mother soothe her. But she was across the country.

And Drew? He might as well be, too.

23

A LOVER, NOT A FIGHTER

Madison reached out and patted Kate's hand. "I'm sure it wasn't as bad as you think it was," she said.

Kate shook her head and dug her hand into the bowl of tortilla chips. "It was worse. You're on this stage, but it feels like you're in some corporate conference room. No one's having a good time. No one's drinking a beer. There are no good vibes at all. These people aren't there to party; they're there to *judge* you."

Madison moved the bowl out of Kate's reach. Kate had eaten half a bag of Sesame Blues already, and if she kept going, she'd be too bloated to fit into those Joe's jeans she always wore. "You've got to stop obsessing about it. You'll have another chance to prove yourself." She heard the front door open. "Here comes Carmen," she said quietly.

Kate looked up and groaned. "Awesome. That's exactly what I need."

Madison knew that the roommates had done a good

job avoiding each other recently (until now, apparently). She also knew that Kate was mad at Drew for missing her showcase, and it didn't take a genius to figure out that things weren't going so great in Luke-and-Carmen Land either.

What a whole lot of trouble was brewing! And for once, Madison hadn't been the cause of it. It was almost enough to make her feel nostalgic for the old days, when she made a practice of betraying Jane Roberts almost weekly.

Carmen stopped short when she saw them on the living room couch. "Oh—" she said, and made as if to turn around.

Madison held up a hand. "Wait, Carmen. Don't leave."

Carmen raised an eyebrow. "Why not?"

"Because your roommate here is having a really rough time, and from what I gather things are not particularly amazing for you at the moment, either, so why don't we sit down and hash things out?"

Both Carmen and Kate stared at her. Madison gave a faint smile, and Carmen narrowed her eyes at her, no doubt trying to determine what nefarious reason underlay Madison's sudden burst of concern.

But Madison didn't have a nefarious reason at all. Although she had a slightly self-serving one (nothing wrong with that!). She knew that if Kate and Carmen made up, the lack of drama in their story line would drive Trevor to look elsewhere for stories . . . for instance, to Madison herself.

But she genuinely liked Kate, and seeing her so down

in the dumps was a bummer. And Carmen didn't feel like a threat to her anymore: Her follow-up to her starring movie role, after all, seemed to be wandering around L.A. aimlessly, eating fro-yo with that annoying hanger-on Fawn.

Madison patted a cushion on the couch. "Have a seat, Carm."

Looking very wary, Carmen reluctantly sat. Kate reached toward the chip bowl but Madison pushed it out of her reach again. "Look, you two," she said. "You're fighting over nothing. Kate, Carmen was drunk, and she's really sorry about what she did. Right?" She looked over at Carmen, who nodded. "And honestly, Kate, Carmen kisses everyone."

"Yeah, especially my boyfriends," Kate said.

"I do *not* kiss everyone," Carmen said.

Madison laughed. "Oh, face it, Carm, you're a bit of a kissing slut. But that's part of your charm."

Kate snorted into her hand.

"That is so not true," Carmen said.

Madison shrugged. "I've been reading about you making out with people for years," she said. "Starting with your sweet sixteen at Chateau Marmont, when you tried to plant a big one on Leonardo DiCaprio."

Kate's eyes widened. "You kissed Leonardo DiCaprio?" There was awe in her voice.

And Carmen started laughing. Hard. And then harder, to the point where she was almost gasping for air. "I tried," she gasped. "Oh my God, I'd forgotten all about that.

He looked at me like he thought maybe he should call security."

Madison clapped her hands. "I'm sure you seemed like such a threat in your glitter eye shadow and training bra."

Carmen glanced down at her sizable chest, then made a wry face. "Uh, these girls haven't been in a training bra since I was in sixth grade."

Then Kate started snickering, too, and pretty soon the tension in the room was completely gone, and they were *all* laughing. Madison was looking at Carmen with new respect; it took guts to laugh that hard at yourself.

"The point is," Madison said, when everyone had calmed down, "not that many people out there understand what we're going through, being on a show like ours. We have to stick up for each other. Be there for each other."

Carmen gazed at her thoughtfully. "You are really not the Madison Parker you played on *L.A. Candy*."

Madison glanced at Kate. "It's like I said to Kate: You have to play a role. But also, people change. Whatever. Don't make a big deal out of it."

But Carmen was right. She wasn't the same Madison Parker, it was true. She was as ambitious as old Madison, but she felt different. Madison remembered vowing, as the season's filming began, that she was going to be cold—but it hadn't really worked out that way.

"I am really, really sorry I kissed Drew," Carmen said, looking to Kate. "It was a moment of complete and total stupidity. I don't know what the hell I was thinking."

Kate nodded. "It's okay," she said. "I forgive you. And I'm sorry I told the crew that you had excessive gas."

Carmen's mouth fell open. "You did not!"

"No, I didn't. But I'm going to if you kiss another one of my boyfriends." Then Kate smiled. "And hey, by the way? Lay off those chips, Curtis. Too much sodium isn't good for a growing baby." Then she started cackling.

Carmen threw up her hands in defeat. "My 'baby bump'!" she cried. "How could I have forgotten?" She shook her head. "God, the things people write about me. Did you know that Lily fed a story to *D-Lish*? I'm so glad I'm not hanging out with her anymore."

Kate's eyes widened. "Lily? But she seemed so nice."

"Yeah, and Gaby's boobs seem real," Madison said. "Well, sort of. The point is, you can never know about people."

"Did you confront her?" Kate asked.

Carmen shook her head. "No, I just can't deal right now. I'm pretty sure she also told that I kissed Drew."

For a moment, Madison wished she'd seen the kiss. It would have been such good currency! But she said, "It's all part of the deal you signed on for. Truth or lies—what does it matter to a blogger, when all he cares about is page views? And what do you care, when all you really need is to stay in the spotlight?" She paused. "Although next time you really ought to wear something under a bias-cut dress. Everyone does. It's called Spanx."

"Duly noted," Carmen said.

Pretty soon they were chatting like nothing had ever come between them, and Madison was giving herself a nice mental pat on the back. It was good when people worked things out.

Madison had some things to work out, too. Last week's meeting with Jack Stanbro over at Gallery had been promising, but Jack was looking for a more detailed pitch. He wasn't going to sign her on simply because she was Madison Parker. On the one hand, she was slightly annoyed by this—did anyone ask a Kardashian for a scripted pilot?—but on the other, she appreciated that he took her seriously enough to ask her to flesh out her ideas.

And then there was the Ryan situation. He'd called her several times since their lunch (exactly as she'd wanted him to), and she was holding him at arm's length (exactly as she'd planned to). Things were going fine on that front. But he kept bringing up Charlie. Ryan said that he didn't think Madison was capable of committing to a relationship until she repaired the one she had with her father.

To which Madison had replied: "Good luck finding that jerk."

Her feelings about the situation were more complicated than that, but she didn't want to go into them. She kind of wished they would go away. She wished her love for her father could have vanished right along with him. That would make everything so much simpler.

"Hey." Kate was poking Madison in the ribs. "Did you see that other thing on *D-Lish* the other day—the one that said Carmen was dealing with a spray-tan addiction?"

Carmen's face was in her hands. She looked up a moment later, her cheeks flushed. "This one's not true! I swear, it is so insane. It's like this one blogger totally has it in for me. He's always the one to print the crazy stuff."

Madison held up a hand. "Wait. Everything we're talking about is posted by the same person?"

Carmen nodded. "My sworn enemy," she said. "Jimmy Landis."

"No, he's not your *enemy*," Madison said. "He's someone's contact."

Carmen looked confused. "What do you mean?"

"Someone is calling him with information about you. True, false, it doesn't matter. There's a source in your circle—probably Lily—and they are feeding stories to the writer. I used to do that all the time." (Often for stories about herself—but that would remain her secret.)

Carmen began biting one of her fingernails. "You think Lily did *that*?" she asked.

Madison shrugged. "I wouldn't put it past anyone."

"But why? What's in it for her?"

"Sometimes people pay for info," Madison suggested. "Or maybe Lily's looking to get mentioned as a makeup artist to the stars? Who knows why people do what they do?"

"It wasn't you, was it?" Carmen asked suddenly.

Madison began to laugh. "No. But I'm sure there were moments I would have enjoyed it."

Carmen threw up her hands. "Oh, whatever, I don't want to think about it anymore. Not right now. I'm too tired."

"Fair enough," Madison said. "But you should take care of it. And if you don't want to, find someone who will."

"Like you?" Carmen asked hopefully.

Madison laughed. "I'd love to help, but I've changed. The new Madison is a lover, not a fighter," she said. And even if it wasn't entirely true, she liked the way it sounded.

Later, when she left Kate and Carmen's apartment, with the two of them curled on the couch and catching up on their latest news, Madison went upstairs and called Ryan. She'd had a change of heart. She was tired of playing games. Hadn't he proven that he really did care, and that he wasn't going to disappear? For once in her life she felt like she could trust someone—maybe she could let herself trust him again. She couldn't exactly say that to him, though, so instead she said, "Maybe you're right. Maybe I should talk to Charlie. Not that I know how to find him."

"That's the brave thing to do," Ryan told her. "To be open to talking to him."

She laughed. No, the brave thing to do had been to run away from home and make her way to Los Angeles, the city of dreams. The brave thing had been working as hard as she did to make those dreams come true. Some of them had, too. But she knew she still had a long way to go.

24

DON'T CALL US, WE'LL CALL YOU

INT. COFFEE SHOP; DAY

> LEORA sits at a corner table. Her head is bent
> low as she stares intently at a textbook.
> At a nearby table, NOAH is staring intently at
> LEORA. We see him take in her long, tangled
> hair, her pale, nervous hands. There is
> interest in his eyes—and already, perhaps, the
> spark of desire.

NOAH
Um, excuse me—but is that *Elements of Moral
Philosophy*?

LEORA
(Looking up sharply) What's it to you?
(Looking back down and then mumbling) Why
don't you drink your pumpkin chai latte and
mind your own business?

Carmen bit her lip as she paged through the script. She'd already read it through twice, and while it didn't thrill her, it also wasn't the worst thing she'd ever read. (That was the thriller about the college student who discovers that the kid she's babysitting is in fact a state-of-the-art robot. And it's carrying highly classified information that, in the wrong hands, could bring down the world's financial markets. Talk about dumb with a capital D.)

So Carmen was keeping an open mind about *Hearts on Fire*. She knew that Trevor was anxious for her to sign on to a new project, and she was getting a little restless herself. Restless in a larger, existential sense—there were only so many afternoons she could spend hanging with Fawn—and also right in this moment. She'd been waiting in the small, nondescript room of the casting agent's office for ten minutes, and neither the agent nor the leading man was anywhere in sight.

"What's it to you?" she whispered. "Why don't you drink your pumpkin chai latte and mind your own business?"

Then Noah—already being played by indie darling Matt Benson—would stutter, blush, and ask her who pissed in her decaf soy skinny half-caf.

Today was a chemistry read: Carmen and Matt would be videotaped reading a handful of scenes to see whether or not they'd be believable enemies, then lovers. She looked up in relief as the doorknob turned. *Finally*, something was going to happen around here.

"Hey, Carmen," Matt said, striding in and leaning

down to give her a hug. "How's tricks?"

Carmen almost didn't recognize him. She'd met Matt at a party less than a year ago, when he was new in town, nervous and starstruck. Now he was tanned, toned, and more confident. Why did Hollywood do that to *everyone*?

"Oh, things are great," Carmen said, tapping the script on her lap and feeling suddenly nervous. "Congratulations on getting the part of Noah."

"Thanks, man," Matt said. "I, like, petitioned so hard it was totally embarrassing. I even sent Andrew Flynn a variegated agave cactus."

"A *cactus*?"

Matt nodded. "Yeah, he collects really rare ones. I read about it in *Vanity Fair*."

Carmen was pondering this when Wendy Liston, the casting agent, and Andrew Flynn, the director, entered the room. Suddenly there was a lot of handshaking and earnest smiling (on Carmen's part, anyway—Wendy offered her a tight-lipped semi-grimace and Andrew wasn't smiling at all. Maybe his cactus had died).

Carmen had been hoping for a bit of small talk, to break the ice, but Andrew apparently had a doctor's appointment across town. ("He's a little under the weather," Wendy whispered.) So there was barely enough time for the tech guy to turn on the video camera before Carmen and Matt became Leora and Nate: strangers, then friends, then lovers, and then strangers again, all while drinking an absurd amount of expensive coffee. (It was an indie movie, after all, so it couldn't have a happy ending or anything.)

Carmen easily inhabited the prickly Leora character, and Matt was charming as sweet, sincere Noah. Things were going well, Carmen thought as she flipped to her fourth scene. She still wasn't in love with the script, but she was an *actress*: She could pretend to be.

But then came the scene that mattered most. She and Matt (or Leora and Noah, rather) have a fight, and then they kiss. The fighting part—that was no problem. But when it came time to make up, and to kiss, Carmen and Matt knocked their teeth together. Which hurt. They straightened that out quickly enough, but then Matt's tongue felt giant and clumsy and much too wet. Their noses kept getting in the way of things. And Carmen couldn't forget that Andrew was only three feet away, either, breathing loudly through a stuffed-up nose.

Suddenly the whole audition seemed completely insane to her. Why would anyone sit that close to two people who were making out? Why was Matt such a bad kisser? Had he even remembered to brush his teeth that morning? Why did the script have so much *coffee* in it? Was it some kind of product placement deal with Starbucks?

She broke the kiss off too early, and after that, Andrew ended the audition. He seemed to be trying to hide his disappointment. But it was definitely a don't-call-us-we'll-call-you (not) sort of farewell. Wendy told Carmen she'd done just fine, but Carmen knew better.

She also knew that if they actually *did* call, she wouldn't pick up the phone. She wasn't going to kiss Matt Benson again for all the booties in Barneys.

The one bright spot of the whole disaster? At least the *Fame Game* cameras hadn't been around to capture it.

Fawn met her outside the office. "So?" she demanded, jumping up from the bottom step. "How was it?"

"Oh my God," Carmen gasped. "It started out fine but then it got *awful*. I was terrible—but Matt Benson has the worst breath in the world. I'm ninety-nine percent sure he had an onion bagel for breakfast." Carmen did a face-palm, and then began to laugh.

Fawn nudged her with a bony elbow. "Oh, poor you! Kissing hot guys!"

"Yeah, but one who's in desperate need of a breath mint," Carmen said, reaching into her purse and pulling out a box of Tic Tacs. "Why didn't I hand him these?" She paused as a young girl, a casting intern most likely, passed by on her way out, probably to fetch one of the fancy coffees that Andrew Flynn was clearly obsessed with. Carmen tipped a few Tic Tacs into her palm, then held out the box to Fawn. "And Andrew Flynn does *not* understand personal space. He was practically sitting on my lap. Whoever is going to have to work with that bunch—well, I feel sorry for her."

Fawn tucked her arm through Carmen's. "Oh, to have your Champagne problems! Speaking of which, let's go get cocktails and forget all about it," she said.

Carmen threw her head back and laughed. "That sounds like an excellent idea," she said.

"So you're not going to audition for the robot baby film, I take it," Cassandra said the next night, winking at Carmen. She was stirring a pot of red sauce on the stove and sipping wine from a goblet nearly as large as a fishbowl.

Carmen shook her head as she chopped olives for the salad. "Nope. I also passed on the *re*-remake of *Texas Chainsaw Massacre*."

"And the one starring that guy from the kickboxing movies," Fawn added. She'd invited herself along for dinner, and she was supposed to be peeling carrots, but she seemed to be incapable of operating a peeler.

Carmen wondered if Fawn had ever done a moment's housework. "Have you ever peeled a carrot before?" she finally asked.

Fawn looked at her in surprise. "Of course not. What do you think cooks are for?"

Cassandra raised her eyebrows at Carmen when Fawn wasn't looking. Neither Cassandra nor Philip had ever forgiven Fawn for letting Carmen take the shoplifting fall. Philip, especially, thought Fawn was a spoiled Bel Air drama queen. Cassandra, though, found her amusing. Fawn could certainly be hilarious and charming when she felt like it.

"I heard that Jordan Becker is going to start auditioning

for a role in his next film," Cassandra said, shaking a bit of salt into the pot. "It's not a starring role, but it sounds amazing." She glanced up at Carmen. "Actually, I've already spoken to him about it." She paused. "About you, I mean," she clarified.

Carmen felt a tingle of excitement. "Jordan Becker? I *love* his movies. He's, like, Wes Anderson for people who don't do twee."

Cassandra tasted the sauce, frowned, then tossed in a handful of rosemary. "The role is for a troubled daughter . . . of Maryn Wright and Tom Wade."

Carmen couldn't help it. Her jaw dropped. Maryn Wright and Tom Wade? They were only two of her *favorite actors of all time*. Carmen had grown up watching them, first as they starred in teen dramas, and then as they moved onto rom-coms as well as serious movies. Maryn and Tom turned up in art-house films and thrillers alike. They weren't married in real life, but they'd played opposite each other in so many films that people often thought they were. They'd been friends forever and seemed to have the perfect artistic relationship. (At the height of her obsession, Carmen had read one of those dime-store biographies that Walgreens stocked next to *Tiger Beat* magazine. So she knew kind of a lot about them.)

"Mom, I *have* to audition," Carmen said.

"I thought you weren't going to take any more supporting roles," Fawn interjected.

"Are you kidding? I would be an *extra* for these people,"

Carmen said. "Girl at Laundromat. Supermarket Checker. Whatever."

Cassandra laughed. "I doubt you'll have to take a part *that* small." She gave the sauce one final taste and then nodded. "Time to eat," she said.

Carmen's dad had set the table and was already sitting down and digging into the garlic bread.

"Your mother already tell you about the movie?" he asked, wagging a finger at her. Philip kept saying that he wanted Carmen to enjoy her break, to experience a moment of real life (as much as that was possible when she appeared on a weekly TV show), but Carmen could tell he was excited about the role.

Carmen nodded. "I'm calling my agent tomorrow."

"You don't need to do that," Cassandra said. "I can call up—"

Carmen held up a hand. "Mom, I'll do it the official way," she said. "But thank you."

Once again, her family connections were proving to be extremely helpful, and she could practically hear the nepotism gossip already. Well, as the saying went: *Haters gonna hate.*

Beside her, Fawn speared a lettuce leaf pretty aggressively. "Must be nice," she muttered.

Carmen turned to her. "What?"

"Nothing," Fawn said, smiling brightly.

"Even if it doesn't work out," Cassandra said, "the

audition can't be worse than the one you had for *Hearts on Fire*."

Carmen looked up, startled. "How do you know about that?"

"Google Alert, darling. I need to keep up with my baby when she forgets to return my calls." Cassandra smiled.

"But it happened *yesterday*. How is it news already? And also—who told? There were only three other people in that room!" *And not one of them was Lily*, she thought. Carmen looked questioningly at her friend.

Fawn put her fork down. "Oh my God, it was that girl—the one on the steps," she said. "Remember? She heard everything you were telling me."

Carmen shook her head. "I am so sick of this. Why is everyone up in my business?"

"It's pretty harmless, darling," her mother said.

"It's not like anyone is accusing you of shoplifting any-thing," Philip added, shooting a look at Fawn.

Fawn seemed not to notice. "Personally, I don't under-stand why everything you say is so interesting to the gossip blogs," she said huffily. "Every time I check *D-Lish* it's, like, *Breaking News: Carmen Curtis Drinks a Glass of Water*."

"The one about your supposed kombucha addiction was actually kind of funny," Cassandra said.

"Kombucha," Philip said, making a face. "Can't stand the stuff. Tastes like salad dressing."

"I don't know what kind of kombucha you were

drinking, Dad, but it's not supposed to taste like that. It's delicious."

"Maybe it *was* salad dressing," Cassandra said. "You know how absentminded you can be, dear."

Philip pretended to be offended. "I'm not absent-minded; I'm deeply focused."

"But *not* deeply focused on whatever you're doing at that particular second," Cassandra said. "Remember, Carm, the time he grabbed that glass of what he thought was lemonade?"

"And it was *cold chicken stock*," Carmen said. She and her mother had plenty of stories about the things Philip had eaten or drunk mistakenly.

Philip raised his glass in a toast. "To the beautiful women who tease me mercilessly," he said.

Carmen clinked her glass against his and he winked at her. In a way, these were the times she felt the luckiest. Not when she was having her picture taken on the red carpet, or seeing her face on a two-page spread in *Nylon*, but when she was with her family, and they were laughing, and, barring some weird press rumors, everything seemed like it was all right with the world.

The ringing of a phone cut through their laughter. Carmen reached out to Fawn's iPhone and snatched it away. "No phones at the dinner table," she said. "Family rule."

She glanced down and saw Jimmy Landis's name flashing on the screen. The same name of the reporter whose byline always accompanied the stories about her on *D-Lish*.

Carmen felt the breath leave her lungs in a rush. "Why is Jimmy Landis calling you?" she demanded.

But by the look on Fawn's face, Carmen knew *exactly* why he was calling.

25

A LONG, EMOTIONAL ROAD

Kate held the letter lightly in her hand, turning it over and over but not opening it. She'd recognized the handwriting instantly; her stalker had sent her another love note. She knew she ought to hand it to one of the security guys and ask him to open it. Or else—and this was probably the better idea—she should simply throw it away.

But it was so strange to her that he kept writing, when he'd been chased down the street by SoCal Security after appearing on the Park Towers grounds. She was kind of fascinated by his dedication and persistence. She knew now that there was no way he'd ever get close to her—not with Rick and Mitch and the rest of the security team hanging around 24/7. So why didn't he give up? They were *never* going to be boyfriend and girlfriend the way he so desperately hoped.

Kate sighed. Speaking of boyfriend and girlfriend . . . she rolled over onto her back and stared glumly at the ceiling. She hadn't seen Drew in days, and she was starting to wonder if those terms even described the two of them anymore.

He'd told her that he had a last-minute exam the morning of her showcase, and that he couldn't call her because his phone had died.

She thought that excuse was believable but pretty lame, and told him so. The showcase would have gone completely differently if he'd only bothered to show up—she *knew* it would have. One single exam versus her entire future—was there really any comparison?

But, unfortunately, Drew didn't see it that way.

"I can't drop everything to be your cheerleader anytime you need me, Kate," Drew had said, his voice clipped and angry. "You have to be able to do this stuff on your own. You have the talent—all you need is a little more confidence."

"I don't expect you to drop everything whenever I ask, but you *knew* this particular day was important," she'd retorted. "And you said you'd be there."

"What was I supposed to do? Ditch my class and fail my exam?" Drew had asked. "It's not just the Kate Hayes show, okay? I had a *major test*. I'm going to *college*. And I have a *job*. You seem to have a problem remembering that."

When she didn't say anything—she'd never heard him speak so harshly before and was taken aback—Drew began to apologize. He was such a nice guy, he couldn't help it.

"No, no, you're right," she'd said, waving him off. "It's okay."

She was lying, though; it wasn't okay. She understood that he had a point, but she couldn't forgive him. And they'd hardly spoken since.

But she had to admit, as she got up and went to the kitchen for another spoonful of Chunky Monkey, that the person she was most mad at was herself. She had been dreaming of a career in music ever since she started guitar lessons in grade school. She'd worked hard for over a *decade*, and she'd been given fantastic opportunities. But she'd let her crazy, stupid stage fright get the better of her almost every single time. It was infuriating.

She wondered if she should try that EFT tapping business again, or the yoga class for stress relief that PopTV had filmed her taking during Operation Eliminate Stage Fright. Those things had helped a little, hadn't they? And Kate couldn't overdo it on acupuncture or yoga the way she could—and *had*—on Xanax.

She wished she had someone to talk to about it all. She knew Madison would be more than happy to listen, but Kate sort of wanted someone who wasn't part of the Fame Game, both real and metaphorical. She would have loved to talk to her old roommate, Natalie, for instance. Natalie had always been such a reliable friend, not to mention a good source of advice. But Kate didn't think she ought to unload all her problems on her when she hadn't even called to say hello in weeks.

Kate had been playing phone tag with her sister, but Jess wouldn't be any help in this situation, either. She didn't understand the world of reality TV at all, and her advice would come in the form of annoying sports metaphors. Kate did *not* want to be told to "keep her eye on the ball" or some such athletic-sounding encouragement that didn't apply to anything in her life.

As Kate dipped her spoon into the ice cream carton, she looked down and realized she'd consumed almost an entire pint that afternoon. That meant probably fifty trips into the kitchen, each time to sneak one tiny bite.

She put the ice cream back in the freezer and tossed the spoon into the sink. She needed to get out of the apartment. Immediately.

"Madison's not here," Gaby said, blinking sleepily at Kate. Then she smiled, looking slightly embarrassed. "Sorry. You caught me napping. My therapist says that naps are a time of, like, rejuvenation and healing."

"Sounds nice," Kate said. "And they're a lot better for you than what I did, which was eat almost an entire carton of ice cream without realizing it. Apparently I have the self-control of a four-year-old."

Gaby laughed. "I don't know when Mad'll be back. But you want to come in anyway?"

Kate was disappointed that Madison wasn't home. She'd come to rely on Madison's unique yet often relevant perspective. But she didn't want to hurt Gaby's feelings by turning around and going back downstairs. So she followed her into the penthouse, marveling again at its size.

It was very clean, unlike her own apartment, and Madison was always changing some item of decor or another. (She knew this drove Trevor crazy because of the continuity issues it created, but she didn't seem to care. Or maybe that was the point.) Today there was a new, huge mirror in the shape of a sun above the mantel. Kate caught a glimpse of herself and wondered, once again, if cutting all her hair off had been such a great idea.

"So what's up?" Gaby asked, sitting back down in the place she'd clearly been napping.

Kate perched on top of a brightly printed Missoni pouf. "I'm a little stressed," she said. "But what else is new?" She gave Gaby a careful look. "What about you? How are things . . . since, you know?"

Gaby pulled her hair into a ponytail, then let it fall to her shoulders, and then pulled it back again. She looked at her hands as if they belonged to someone else. "Sorry. I also have a lot of nervous energy. I guess it wasn't clear to anyone, though, because of the pills." She began to braid her dark hair. "But I'm actually doing really good," she said. "Things are different, of course, but they're better. I don't wake up unable to remember what I did the night before, so that's good."

Kate nodded. Yes, retaining memory was definitely a step in the right direction. But she wasn't sure Gaby was staying quite as sober as she was supposed to. "Did I hear that your parents are in town?"

Gaby frowned—or tried her best to, through the

Botox. "They've been threatening to pull me from the show, but so far I've managed to keep them from doing it." Then she gazed at her toes and sighed. "I mean, sometimes it's actually a lot harder for me than I like to admit, but that doesn't mean I want to give it all up."

She looked so lost in that moment that Kate almost got up and hugged her. Instead she said softly, "Gaby, if you're really that unhappy, why don't you leave? Is it really worth the pain?"

Gaby hugged one of the throw pillows against her chest. "Yes," she said, her voice strong again. "This is what I want, Kate. Do you know what people would give to have this opportunity? *Everything*. All I need to do is hold it together through the end of filming."

Kate said, "Actually, what you need to do is hold it together for the rest of your *life*, Gab. Filming isn't a reason to stay sober. Taking care of yourself is."

Gaby laughed. "I know. I've never been very good at that, I guess."

Kate didn't say anything. She was glad that Gaby seemed to grasp what she'd done to herself in the name of celebrity. But would she cancel the cosmetic surgeries she'd lined up post-season? Would she stop seeing Jay? Because it seemed to Kate like not popping pills was only the beginning of Gaby's road to healing.

Kate stretched herself out on the carpeted floor, with her head on the pouf. It was a surprisingly comfortable position, and suddenly she was very, very tired. "What does your therapist say about naps again?" Kate asked sleepily.

"They're healing, physically and emotionally," Gaby said. She laughed. "We've got a spare bed, you know, if you can't make it back to your place."

Kate sighed. "I just want to close my eyes. . . ."

"You dropped something," Gaby said.

Kate felt around on the floor and found the letter from her stalker. "Oh, right," she said. "I was trying to decide whether or not to read the latest creepy stalker letter."

"I always open my mail," Gaby said. "But I don't get as much as you guys. You should see the piles Madison gets."

And so Kate opened her letter and scanned down the page. Halfway down, she paled.

"What?" Gaby asked. "What is it?"

Kate looked up at her. She didn't know whether to laugh or cry. So she read the letter out loud. " 'Dear Kate, Being in love with you has been a long, emotional road for me. But all good things must come to an end. My heart now belongs to Miley Cyrus. Best wishes.' " She met Gaby's eye. "My stalker," she said, holding up the letter. "I think he broke up with me."

And then she laughed harder than she'd laughed in forever.

26

LOOK WHAT THE CAT DRAGGED IN

Madison made one final check of the room: the flowers arranged perfectly, the plate of bagels and croissants waiting on the dining room table. (Unlike their hostess, the guests didn't worry about carb consumption.) The coffee was steaming inside the carafes Madison had ordered from Coffee Bean.

A text came in from Ryan. BE THERE IN FIVE. Madison took a deep breath. OK C U SOON, she wrote back.

A few days after she had called him, Madison and Ryan had begun spending time together again. Not much—but enough to make Madison wonder if things might be heading back toward the romantic. (Which she wanted? Didn't want? Her feelings changed by the hour.)

They'd taken walks in out-of-the-way places and drives up PCH on sunny, windy days. It had been nice. Beyond nice, in fact. They joked and laughed and traded stories about their jobs. But they never talked about what was going on with Them. Ryan didn't seem to be seeing anyone, and Madison certainly wasn't into any of her *Fame Game* dates, but the situation remained unclear. Were they friends? A semi-couple? Or merely friendly exes? Neither spoke about it. They held hands sometimes, but they hadn't kissed. As tempting as that sounded, it was a step Madison wasn't ready to take.

Now Madison wiped an invisible speck of dust from the table. Everything looked perfect, and she was pleased. But she was also slightly annoyed at herself for caring, for going to all this trouble. Did the situation really warrant it? Should she feel so nervous and apprehensive?

Well, yes, as a matter of fact. Ryan was coming over for the first time in forever—and he was bringing Charlie Wardell, Madison's father, with him.

How Ryan had found him, Madison still wasn't sure. Something about Ryan's dad having friends in high places. But if Madison knew anything about her father, it was that he didn't frequent the high places—so really, that explanation told her nothing.

Not that it mattered. Charlie had been gone, and now he was back; *that* was what mattered. Apparently he had been holed up somewhere in Wyoming, living in a borrowed trailer and fixing engines for under-the-table wages. He was no longer on the run, but he wasn't exactly looking to be found, either.

Madison had mixed feelings about Ryan's meddling. He'd stuck his nose in her family business before, trying to broker peace between her and Sophie—which was sort of annoying. On the one hand, if it weren't for him, who knew when she'd see her dad again? If ever. Maybe he'd show up on her wedding day, looking rumpled and apologetic and bearing a gift he'd shoplifted from Nordstrom. On the other hand, Madison's relationship with her father was *her* business, and why her former boss and boyfriend thought he should make it his was baffling.

Madison sighed. There was no sense in going over it again. What was done was done.

And she could hear the two of them coming down the hall right now.

She opened the door before they could knock. Ryan looked handsome and perfectly clean-cut in a dark gray sweater, especially when compared with Charlie. Try as her dad might, he never looked like he hadn't slept in his clothes for a couple of days. Of course, for all Madison knew, he had.

Ryan leaned in and gave her a warm hug. She squeezed him back tightly and breathed in his familiar, comforting smell of clean laundry and bar soap. She sort of wished they could stand like that, pressed together, forever. But it was time to deal with her father. She pulled away and turned toward Charlie.

He gazed at her with eyes that looked like they might overflow with tears. "Look what the cat dragged in," he said softly. He stepped forward as if to hug her, too, but then hesitated.

"Please, come inside," Madison said. Her heart was

racing and she was finding it hard to breathe. She thought of herself as so tough—but seeing Charlie always, *always* reminded her that in some ways she wasn't. That there was a part of her that would forever be little Madelyn Wardell from Armpit Falls, who only wanted her daddy to stick around and take care of her.

Charlie and Ryan sat at the dining room table and Madison poured them coffee. (She silently wished she had a shot of whiskey to dump into hers.)

Charlie reached for a croissant and broke it into two, scattering crumbs all over his pants and the floor. He laughed nervously. "Seems like I make a mess wherever I go, don't it?" he said.

"Literal and figurative," Madison said. She couldn't help it—she was so glad to see Charlie again, but she also wanted to reach across the table and strangle him.

Ryan, of course, was ready to play peacemaker. "Charlie and I have done a lot of talking," he said. He looked at the croissants but didn't take one. "And it sounds like he's really turning things around. He's got a steady job. He's paid off his debts, and he's saving money."

Charlie nodded. "First time in my life I have a savings account," he said. "Every penny in there has your name on it, Maddy."

Madison sipped her coffee. "Thank you, but I don't need your money," she said. Her voice came out cooler than she meant it to.

"For the necklace," Charlie said. He twisted his hands

together nervously. "I suppose you figured this out, seeing as how you're so smart, but I was in trouble. I had gambling debts that got so big they were going to bury me. That necklace—well, it freed me."

Madison frowned. "But how? You can't take something like that to a pawn shop. I mean, it's not some half-carat solitaire from Kay Jewelers."

Charlie gave a little laugh. "No, ma'am, you can't pawn a necklace like that. But Leeann, who's the wife of the guy I owed, she loves nothing better than diamonds. She's like a crow—anything sparkly, she's got to have it. So she took one look at that necklace and she said to her husband, 'You tell Charlie we're even now.' And that's what he did." He gazed at Madison, his blue eyes pleading. "I'm so sorry I did what I did. But I knew she'd love that thing. I was never going to be able to come up with the money, but I could give her that necklace."

"So you planned the whole thing," Madison said, frowning.

Charlie shook his head. "Oh no, honey, not like that, no. I was living here, trying to decide whether to change my name and run, or be with my daughters, or give myself up, or what. But then I saw the necklace and it all became clear to me. It was a way out."

"I don't suppose you stopped to think what it would mean for me," Madison snapped. "How it would ruin my reputation. How I'd be the one to clean up your mess. Just like I did when you left us years ago." She could feel her fists clenching. She wanted to stay cool, but it was impossible. She was so damn *tired* of being abandoned by her father.

"Maddy, you have to believe me when I say I had no idea the trouble I was causing. I honestly thought insurance would cover the necklace. I never would have done it if I knew . . ."

Charlie put his head in his hands. He was silent, and his shoulders shook.

He's crying, Madison thought. *The bastard is actually crying.*

Ryan reached over and placed his hand over her clenched fist. "He's trying to do right," he whispered. "You mean the world to him, and you always have."

"He has the worst way of showing it," Madison said back, not caring if Charlie heard. She hoped that if she let her anger out, she could be done with it.

The doorbell rang again, and Ryan shot her a wary, almost nervous look. "I also told Sophia he was coming," he admitted.

Madison pulled her hand away. "God," she said, "you don't know when to stop, do you?"

"He's her father, too," Ryan said gently. "She loves him. He loves her. Don't you think she deserves to be here?"

Madison sighed and got up to let her sister in, praying that she hadn't brought the cameras with her. Ryan had told Madison that he was working through his fear of publicity—he realized how quickly the attention went away, how small his story was compared to the big world of celebrity news—but she didn't think he was ready for the PopTV crew. And nor was she. Not today.

She opened the door and braced herself for the onslaught. But it was only Sophie, who immediately rushed past her, arms outstretched, calling "Daddy, Daddy!"

She practically threw herself at Charlie's feet. "Oh, I missed you so much. You have no idea how hard it's been for us."

Madison rolled her eyes to the ceiling and then nudged her sister with her foot. *Not* gently. "Get up, Soph," she said. "You didn't bring the cameras, so you can save the Oscar-worthy performance."

Sophie looked up at Madison with narrowed eyes and then turned back to her father. "We really have been *desperate* for news."

Charlie reached out and smoothed Sophie's hair from her face. "I missed you, honey," he said. "I thought about you every day."

Madison sat back down at the table. "Maybe you could have sent another postcard," she said pointedly.

"Hey, you guys are all together now," Ryan said in an attempt to keep everyone positive. "Let's take a second to appreciate that. A reunion."

Sophie was still half on Charlie's lap, but Charlie didn't take his eyes off Madison. "Honey, I will spend the rest of my life regretting the hardship I've caused you. And I'm going to do everything in my power to make things better." He wiped a tear from his cheek. "I want to be a part of your life. Please, please, will you let me?"

Madison didn't say anything right away. She'd heard him say things like this before. Would she be a fool to believe him this time?

Yes, she would.

But she knew she was probably going to do it anyway.

She felt a small smile twitching at the corner of her mouth. "If you want to be my dad," she said, "you need to act like it. No more stealing. Ever. For one thing, it's illegal, and for another, you're horrible at it. Seriously."

"I'll tell everyone I took the necklace," he said.

"No!" Madison cried. "What's done is done." She wondered if Charlie understood *anything*. She couldn't go back to the press and admit she'd lied. It would ruin everything. She'd lied under oath! "It's all been taken care of, so we leave it alone now."

Charlie nodded. "I'm so sorry," he whispered.

"And another thing," Madison said. "Family is not about running away. It's about being there for people." She looked over at Ryan, who was nodding.

She realized, maybe for the first time, how much he had been there for her. How, when they were together, *he* had been her family. She reached out and took his hand, wrapping her fingers through his. "Thank you," she mouthed.

And when Ryan smiled at her, she leaned over the table and kissed him on the cheek.

It startled him, she could tell. But that was all right. She thought there was a chance they'd figure things out.

27

A BRIGHT SIDE TO EVERYTHING

Carmen had arrived early for her audition for Jordan Becker's new movie, feeling confident and excited. Her agent had already had a promising off-the-record chat with the director. Supposedly Jordan thought Carmen could be the perfect rebellious teenage daughter of Maryn Wright and Tom Wade. Supposedly he'd been wanting to work with her ever since he'd seen her in *The Long and Winding Road*.

Carmen had needed good news like this to counteract the depressing realization of Fawn's betrayal. For months (months!) her alleged bestie had Jimmy Landis on speed dial so she could feed him gossip. Carmen couldn't believe how someone so close to her—and someone who still *owed* her, big time, for Tanktopgate—could be so cruel.

And then there was Lily. Turns out her only betrayal was telling Fawn about Carmen's supposed interest in Jonah Byrne of Sadly Sarah. Carmen had frozen her out for no reason, and the poor thing probably still didn't know why.

Laurel had been unsurprised when Carmen revealed

that Fawn was the source of all the bizarre and false information. "Personally, I always thought she seemed a little backstabby," Laurel had said.

"But why? I don't get it," Carmen had said.

"Who knows? But I'll do a little digging," Laurel promised. "Maybe we can get to the bottom of it."

And Carmen had thanked her profusely, feeling guilty for ever having wondered if Laurel was the source of the intel.

Now, as the time for her audition approached, Carmen steeled herself. *No more thoughts of Fawn,* she told herself. *Think only of the awesome role you're about to get.*

The cameras were ready now. "Speed," called the sound guy. "Action," called someone else.

And Carmen, with a clear and optimistic mind, began to walk. The PopTV cameras filmed her entering the studio and meeting Jordan. He had a very firm handshake and a warm smile. She couldn't believe that he'd allowed PopTV to film. Should she take that as another sign of his confidence in her? Surely he wouldn't want to appear on TV with an actress he didn't respect. . . .

Carmen was going to read opposite two of his assistants, who would be reading the roles of Maryn, Tom, and assorted other bit players. It felt informal this way—almost like auditioning for her high school plays. Of course there were cameras all over, but she was used to them.

Carmen's dad liked to talk about how he could hear less than five seconds of a band's music and simply *know* they'd be a hit. It was like some sixth sense, he'd say—a secret voice whispering, *These guys have it.*

That morning, Carmen heard that secret voice whispering in her ear. It said, *You're going to nail this.* And because of this, Carmen sat up straighter. Her voice projected louder. She *became* Stella Wray, the bright, troubled daughter of a dancer and an architect. Even though the assistants did a terrible job of reading their lines, Carmen hit every single one of hers. She felt so good about her performance she wanted to act out the whole movie right then and there.

When Jordan said that he'd seen enough, Carmen turned to him and smiled a megawatt smile. She couldn't help it—she was suddenly elated.

This was what she wanted. A smart drama, with indie credibility and Hollywood money, starring two of her favorite actors. If she got the role, she might just die of happiness.

"I'll be talking to you soon," Jordan said, enfolding her hand with his. "I have a good feeling about this."

And Carmen did, too.

She felt like she was floating as she made her way to her car. PopTV made sure to capture her cheerful exit, complete with a few hopeful, optimistic looks directed toward the movie studio's giant logo. (Carmen wondered what music Trevor would pick for those shots—Kate's new song "Gonna Make It"? Or something that had climbed a little higher on the charts? She'd have to remember to watch the episode to find out.) Then she handed her mike pack to Laurel and waved good-bye for the day.

Safe in her car, Carmen pulled out her phone. Now that her career felt like it was getting back on track, she had some personal business to attend to.

First, she texted Lily. It was time to clear the air between the two of them. *Past* time, in fact; Carmen should have called her the moment she saw Jimmy's name on Fawn's screen. But she hadn't: She'd spent too much time feeling sorry for herself over the bad press and the Drew situation.

She vowed she would make it up to Lily. She'd hook her up with new clients—starting with Cassandra (who needed a backup when her longtime makeup artist was unavailable). Meanwhile, the awful Fawn would be stuck doing voice-overs for feminine hygiene commercials until the end of time.

SORRY, CRAZY BUSY LATELY, Carmen texted. WOULD LOVE TO SEE YOU SOON. LET'S TALK! BRUNCH?

Carmen took a deep breath. Now it was time to reach out to Luke. Face-to-face—to the degree that was possible when an ocean separated them. She reapplied her lipstick and ran her fingers through her shining hair before dialing his number. Then she set the phone on the dash and waited for him to pick up.

After a few rings, he did. His face was pixilated at first, and then it resolved into handsome clarity. "Hey, what a surprise," he said. She couldn't read his expression at all.

"Hey, yourself," she said. Carmen took another long, deep breath. "Listen, I know we've sort of talked about this already, but I wanted to say again how sorry I am about the whole Drew mess. It was such a little thing—I don't know how it turned into such a big deal."

Luke smiled faintly. "I'll admit I was hurt when I read about it. But I also know that I'm thousands of miles away, and I can't expect you to be waiting for me—"

"But you can," Carmen interrupted. "I mean, I don't want to date Drew. I don't want to date anyone but—" She was going to say "you," but apparently it was Luke's turn to interrupt.

"Well, actually," Luke said. "I've been meaning to talk to you about this." He looked away for a moment, and Carmen saw his strong profile on her screen. Then he turned back and met her eyes. "I've actually started seeing someone here," he said.

Carmen gasped. "What?" Then immediately she tried to play it cool. "You are, huh? Wow, okay. Who is it?"

"My costar," Luke said. "Antonia David."

"Who?"

Luke didn't seem to hear the question. "Neither of us were looking for anything, but then suddenly we really hit it off." He shrugged helplessly. "I know you and I left things sort of . . . up in the air, and of course I'd never want to hurt you . . ." He trailed off.

Carmen honestly didn't know how she felt, although she was definitely leaning toward hurt and insulted. But she didn't want Luke to know that. "Wow, okay, no, that's great, I'm really happy for you, totally," she said. The words tumbled over themselves. She suddenly regretted calling him on FaceTime. She knew her expression wasn't matching her words. (Apparently, when it came to life, Carmen wasn't *quite* as good an actress.) "I mean, it's not like we can actually date when we're across the world from each other." She laughed, but to her it sounded hollow.

"I really think you're great, Carmen," Luke said.

She nodded. "Sure, of course." *Just not great enough,* she thought. *Not as great, say, as Antonia David.* Carmen didn't even know who Antonia David was. She made a mental note to Google stalk this chick later.

She flipped her hair back and offered Luke a bright smile. "Well, I should get going," she said. "Places to go, people to see . . ."

Luke smiled back. Was there a hint of sadness in it? Carmen wished there was, but she sort of didn't think so. "Take care of yourself, love," he said.

As she drove toward her apartment, Carmen began to cry. The day had started out so perfectly, and then Luke had to go and ruin it. It wasn't even that she loved him, or was waiting for him to come back to her (not *really*)—but rejection sucked. There were no two ways about it.

She pulled down the photo-booth strip of the two of them that she had tucked into the visor and tossed it onto the floor. She would delete his number as soon as she got home. (She should have done it immediately, but now she was driving, and she wasn't risking an accident or ticket over that on-set floozy.) She thought of his cute little place in Venice and wished that all of his plants would die.

A week ago she would have called Fawn, but that back-stabber was on the do-not-call list, probably for the rest of her life. Carmen could have tried Lily again, but since she iced her out without telling her why, it would seem a little weird to barrage her with texts and phone calls. (But why hadn't Lily responded to the text she'd sent? Lily kept her iPhone charged and on her person constantly, and her normal response time was about ten nanoseconds.) Carmen bit her lip, hoping she hadn't ruined things with her, too.

At least Carmen and Kate had patched things up, thanks to Madison's intervention. (Carmen was still marveling over *that* unexpected turn of events.) But she didn't want to test their shaky friendship by calling to complain about Kate's ex. And since Carmen hadn't seen Drew walking around in a towel for weeks, and all her leftovers had remained untouched, she had to wonder if things weren't a little off with Krew lately.

She tried to reassure herself that none of this was her fault. This was a crazy, high-pressure life, and not everyone was cut out for it. She remembered Drew's reaction when she first told him about being approached by Trevor Lord. Drew had said it was a bad idea, and that Carmen was "above" reality TV.

She wasn't "above" anything, she'd argued. A TV network thought she was interesting enough to feature on a major show—how was that *anything* but flattering? She wanted to make her own way, and *The Fame Game* had seemed like a great way to do it. And it was! But sometimes it seemed like living this sort of second life had swept away all her real friends. And at the same time, it had made her wonder: If they were so quick to go, were they real friends in the first place?

Carmen pulled into the parking lot of her apartment building, tired but still agitated. She decided that a quick soak in the hot tub would make her feel better. Maybe she could persuade Kate to come sit by the pool with her and share a glass of wine. (There were probably a hundred people living in Park Towers, yet no one but the *Fame Game* girls ever seemed to use the pool. It was weird, but Carmen liked it that way.)

She was walking up to the entrance when a figure stepped out from behind one of the giant potted palms. Carmen flinched—was it Kate's stalker again? She thought he'd moved on!

But, no, it was Fawn, with a desperate look on her face. "Carmen," she began, "I'm so sorry. I can explain—"

Carmen glared at her. "I really don't want to talk to you." She'd hear the explanation—if there was one—from Laurel.

"Please, Carm," Fawn said. "Just listen to me."

"There's literally nothing you can say that I want to hear," Carmen said coldly. "Now please leave. This is private property, and you are trespassing." When Fawn made no move to go, Carmen added, "I'll go get security. They're playing cards in my apartment." It wasn't true anymore, but what Fawn didn't know wouldn't hurt her.

And then she swept past Fawn and headed for the elevator. She didn't have to turn around to know that Fawn was leaving. As the doors closed she watched Fawn's car pulling away.

Good riddance, she thought. Then she smiled, thinking of tampons dancing the Macarena, and the last words she'd ever hear from Fawn: *Who says your period can't be fun?*

28

THAT IS GENIUS

Trevor had delivered the notice earlier that morning. Stephen Marsh: the last producer hired and the first to be fired. Trevor was never certain it would work out with Stephen—after all, he'd been hired as a favor to Trevor's boss—but he certainly couldn't have predicted the mess Stephen would get himself into in a matter of months.

His less-than-impressive job performance aside, he was actually sleeping with a member of the cast.

"No points for guessing who," Trevor had said to Laurel.

"The blond sociopath," Laurel said.

At that, Trevor had laughed mirthlessly. Laurel loved to remind him of the other fun news he'd gotten recently: Sophia's personality test results had come in, and she was somewhere between borderline personality disorder and histrionic personality disorder.

In layman's terms, she was either bat-shit crazy, or utterly desperate, or both. Trevor had nodded as he read;

yes, this diagnosis certainly explained some things.

He had decided to wash his hands of her, too. With Gaby back on track (mostly) and her parents dispatched back to their McMansion, Trevor was relieved to not have to hunt for an additional cast member. In fact, Gaby's story line was getting bigger and more interesting. He'd finally gotten her an audition for *Dancing with the Stars*, and he was already filming her practicing. She was surprisingly talented—and unexpectedly dedicated. She'd practiced for five hours straight the other day. And while she might have been slipping with her sobriety recently, her commitment to dancing had nipped that potential problem in the bud. Trevor also had gotten her into a new therapy group, at her parents' insistence, which was probably helpful, too. How he wished he could film *that*!

He wondered what Madison would think about Sophia being let go. Their relationship was always a bit of a mystery to him. They had their sweet moments, but for the most part Sophia was nothing but a thorn in her sister's side. Who would have thought Madison would put up with Sophia as long as she had? Was it family loyalty? Or was Sophia in possession of yet another secret Madison didn't want to get out?

Trevor wished that were the case, but he doubted it. Sophia had already outed Madison as the pudgy brunette from a trailer park—what worse secret could there be?

"Maybe Madison's actually a man," Laurel had said, with a completely straight face.

They'd had a good laugh over that one.

He was actually chuckling about it again when Laurel burst into his office, knocking her hip on the doorjamb in her hurry to get to him.

"Are you all right?" Trevor asked, watching her rub what was certainly going to be a large bruise.

Laurel ignored the question. "Sophia's filed a sexual harassment suit," she said breathlessly.

Trevor stared at her. "A sexual harassment suit?" he repeated. His brain seemed to be working slower than normal all of a sudden. "On what grounds? Her relationship with Stephen was consensual. And anyway, I fired him already."

Laurel sank into the chair opposite his desk. "No, Trevor," she said. "The suit isn't accusing Stephen of sexual harassment. It accuses *you*."

Trevor sucked in his breath. "What?"

But Laurel didn't repeat herself. She knew he'd heard.

Trevor jumped out of his chair. "That is the most ridiculous thing I've ever heard! She really is insane!"

"Yes, we've confirmed that," Laurel said. "Although maybe a little too late."

Trevor stalked over to the window and stared out at the L.A. skyline. The palm trees, waving in the wind, the stocky shapes of the buildings, the distant hills: They all seemed to taunt him. Suddenly he turned back to Laurel. "Actually," he said, "that is genius." He smiled wryly and began to shake his head.

Laurel raised an eyebrow. "Pardon?"

"She's accusing me of assault because she can't be fired if I'm being investigated for a crime against her." He hit his palm on the window frame. "Stephen must have told her that he'd been fired. She saw the ax above her own head. And then she figured out a way to stop it."

Trevor couldn't believe it. He knew that he was innocent, and that this would be quickly proven. But in the meantime, the court of public opinion could make his life a lot less pleasant.

"I'm sorry," Laurel whispered.

Trevor waved her away. He picked up the phone to call his lawyer. This BS was going to cost him. He only wished there was a way for him to make Sophia pay.

29

A LITTLE BIT BRIGHTER

Kate waited at the back of the room, Lucinda gripped tightly in her hand. There were more people than she'd expected. The last time she played an open mic there were about twenty people in the audience; tonight there was at least three times that. Maybe the guy who played the Jackson 5 covers—which sounded totally weird on an acoustic guitar—had finally developed the following he'd been working so hard for. (He'd given Kate and everyone else his card about a million times, while begging them to go to Vimeo to see the new videos he'd made.) Or maybe word had gotten out that this was the best place to see up-and-coming talent. Certainly no one was expecting to see Kate Hayes—in part because people with hit singles rarely played open mics, and in part because she'd signed up simply as Katherine (which she otherwise never used) and pulled a knit cap over her now-signature platinum pixie.

Kate reached up and touched her nose, which felt slightly sunburned. She had taken a long walk that morning—solo, no cameras (except for the little Nikon she'd brought to take snapshots). She'd been thinking hard about her life, and whether or not it looked like the one she thought she ought to be living, and she decided that it didn't. Not quite.

Back during last season's Operation Cure Stage Fright, a therapist had given Kate an exercise: "Think of three things you're grateful for," she'd said. "Examine them, celebrate them—and then let them go. Now think of three things that bother you. Examine them, evaluate them—and then let them go, too. Feel how your mind becomes clear, focused, and unafraid."

The woman seemed so certain of her advice, but Kate hadn't bothered to take it. She'd simply popped a couple anti-anxiety pills and headed to the yoga class Trevor was making her attend (on film). Yoga didn't involve thinking, after all, and Kate was so relaxed by then she could bend herself like a pretzel.

But, six months later, as she hiked through Griffith Park under the sunny March sky, she wondered if she ought to give the woman's exercise a try. Kate's mind was an agitated jumble—maybe it would help, and it certainly couldn't hurt.

So as Kate walked along the dirt path, she began to remember: the sound of her voice through the monitors at Studio Nineteen; the times she'd lost her nerve onstage; the disastrous showcase; the sweet, lonely feeling of playing Lucinda late at night in an otherwise empty room; the magical feeling when a song began to come together in her mind. She went further back, remembering the finger exercises her dad made her do, the silly songs he made up on the spot to sing along. *There once was a frog / who thought he was a dog / so he tried to eat a bone; / but it stuck in his throat / so he jumped on a boat / and paddled right back home . . .*

Kate felt the prick of tears in her eyes. It had been a while since she'd thought about her dad. Maybe that was the way life went; in order to keep moving forward you had to not look back. Or maybe, somewhere along the way, she'd lost touch with who she really was and what she wanted to be.

She didn't want to be KATE HAYES, that name in lights, surrounded by handlers and stylists and security specialists. Not really (though she really needed a stylist—or so said Madison). Kate wanted to be *herself*—with her strawberry-blond waves and her admittedly sloppy style. She wanted her songs to make people feel things. She didn't want to be disguised behind layers of digital sound. She didn't want her music to be Auto-Tuned the way she had allowed her life to be.

She wished her dad were still around to give her advice; he was always so good at it. But she thought she knew what he'd say: *Focus on the music, Katie. The* music *is what matters. Everything else comes and goes, and it's not something to worry about.*

Kate felt a surge of hope. She knew how to focus on the music. It meant forgetting her manager and her chances for another showcase for the time being. It meant ignoring Trevor's rules about "going rogue" and playing surprise shows without PopTV cameras; it meant doing it by herself, her way. Without anyone to help her.

Not even Drew.

Maybe Taylor Swift had said it best: "People haven't always been there for me, but music always has."

And *music* was why Kate had moved to L.A., against her mother's wishes; not because she wanted to be famous, but because she wanted to write songs that people would hear. She wanted people to smile when they heard them come on the radio. She knew how corny it sounded, but she wanted to try to make the world a little bit brighter.

Now, as the singer who was on right before her began his final song, Kate took a deep breath. She wasn't thinking about her performance, though—she was thinking about melody. The way one note built on another and the next, and the way something beautiful could be conjured right out of the air. She thought, again, of her dad, but this time she smiled.

When she heard her name called out, she walked to the stage. In the front row sat Madison, who waved and blew her a kiss. Beside her, Ryan gave Kate a big smile. Kate looked at him a little surprised; she hadn't been expecting him. But she was glad he was there for Madison's sake. Kate thought he was good for Madison, even if Madison sometimes claimed she wasn't so sure.

When Kate took her place in the center of the stage,

the room went silent for a moment. Then she heard some-one whisper, "Is that Kate Hayes?" The words went flying around the room, and in seconds her cover was blown. Kate adjusted herself on the wooden stool and offered them a smile. "Hey, everyone," she said softly, and immediately the applause was thunderous.

She could feel their anticipation, their high spirits. She wasn't going to let them down. She leaned forward into the microphone. "This is a song that I used to sing with my dad," she said, and then she began to play.

"God, I wish I could have gotten that on tape," Madison said later, as she handed Kate the bowl of steaming, salty microwave popcorn. It was just the two of them now back at Kate's apartment. "It'd get a million hits in five minutes on YouTube. Those new songs were amazing. And you! You didn't even screw up at *all*!"

Kate laughed. Leave it to Madison to make a compli-ment sound backhanded, even when it wasn't. But she was feeling too good to mind—and anyway, what Madison had said was true. The open mic had gone even better than she'd dared hope. "Finally I didn't humiliate myself," she said, grabbing a handful of buttery popcorn.

Madison delicately took a single kernel, inspected it, and then tossed it into her mouth. "Not bad," she said.

"Have more," Kate urged.

"Don't you know me better than that?" Madison asked, faking a stern look.

"Well, people change," Kate said. "What if I've become a singer that can actually perform?"

"Well, if tonight is any indication, you are well on your way. But I will never be a person who eats carbs. I tried that once, remember? And then I had to get lipo."

"How could I forget?" Kate asked. "I waited on you hand and foot. Like a servant!" She grinned and reached for more popcorn.

Madison pooh-poohed this. "I don't remember the servant part. I seem to recall you spending most of your afternoons with me mooning over Drew."

At that, Kate's face fell.

"What?" Madison asked. "Did I say something wrong?"

Kate shook her head. "No, it's not you. It's just . . ." She sighed. "I don't think Drew likes Rocker Kate as much as he liked Regular Kate. It's almost like there's a part of him that wants me to be on the *verge* of success forever—but not actually ever reach it."

Madison frowned. "That's weird. Are you sure?"

"No," Kate said after a while. "I don't really know. Maybe I'm telling myself that to explain why things are so off between us. He said he thought we should take a break. And that it was because he wanted me to be able to focus on my career, but that doesn't make sense, because he was *helping* me. Why would he need to run away?"

Madison leaned back and put her long, slender legs on the coffee table. "Who knows," she said. "I gave up on the idea that I'd ever understand what a guy was think-ing." She paused. "Except for Jay. I always know what he's thinking. 'Dude. Where's the Jim Beam? Bro, do you like my ass tattoo?'"

Kate laughed. "Yeah, I think Drew is a little more complicated than that."

"It's hard not to be," Madison said. "But really, Kate, there are more fish in the sea. How about you have a little rebound fling with one of your security guys? That one with the green eyes is seriously hot." She mimed fanning herself.

"They're all gone," Kate said, feeling even lower. "I didn't tell you that? Even my stalker broke up with me."

"*What?*"

Kate nodded. "He said he's in love with Miley Cyrus now."

Madison was clearly trying not to laugh, and Kate appreciated that. "Someday," Madison said after a moment, "you'll look back on this and laugh."

"I sure hope so," Kate said.

"Anyway, I'm not too sorry that Drew's gone. He's a nice guy, but you can do better. You're free now, Kate."

Free, Kate thought. *In more ways than one.*

30

A LOT OF HISTORY

Carmen slid into the booth across from Drew at Factor's Famous Deli. He looked up from his menu and smiled—a little warily, maybe, but still. It counted.

"I'm not going to kiss you," Carmen said immediately. "So don't worry."

This sparked a sudden burst of laughter. "Hi to you, too," Drew said. "It wasn't a concern, but thanks."

"If you say so. But you gotta admit, you look like you're ready to make a run for the exit." Just for fun, Carmen began to lean toward him, as if she were aiming for another kiss. "Boo," she blurted, and then settled back down in her seat.

"Very funny," Drew said, slightly testily. But then he smiled again. "Do you want to split a sundae?"

Carmen glanced at the menu but didn't open it. This was the diner they'd come to the night they first met Kate. It felt suddenly odd that her roommate wasn't here, too. But she'd made her peace with Kate. Tonight was

242

between Carmen and Drew.

"Sure, why not? But I know what splitting means to you. It means I get two bites and you eat the rest in under five minutes," she teased. (Her waistline could certainly afford a few bites of an ice cream sundae, and now that she knew she wouldn't be reading about her "out-of-control emotional eating," it would taste all the better.)

Drew laughed. "Technically that *is* splitting. I didn't say anything about equal portions."

After the waitress had taken their order—two Diet Cokes and a sundae inexplicably called the Mt. Vesuvius—Carmen turned to Drew, a serious look on her face. "I wanted to tell you in person how sorry I am about what happened at the party."

"Really, Carm, we don't have to talk about it," Drew said. "It's no big deal. It's not like we've never kissed before."

Carmen remembered a party about a year ago, when they had fumblingly made out in someone's basement and then, the next day, pretended as if it had never happened. They'd never quite been able to figure out their feelings for each other, and it seemed like in some ways, that was still the case. She smiled faintly. "Yeah, but when we kissed back then, you weren't seeing anyone. Especially not my roommate."

Drew grimaced, then tried to hide it by taking a quick sip of water.

Carmen eyed him carefully. "You are still seeing her,

right?" She'd certainly wondered, but she hadn't wanted to ask Kate for fear of upsetting her.

Drew looked down at his hands. "I don't know," he admitted. "Not exactly right now. This whole thing with Kate wanting to be a superstar—I'm just not into it. It's not the music I want to make, and all those producers and sound mixers and managers and stuff—they aren't the kind of people I want to hang out with."

"You're her boyfriend, not her manager. You are dating her, not her music. Also, you work at a major record label and probably deal with those people daily."

"Yeah, but I'm in, like, the indie wing. We don't do Katy Perry; we do the Lumineers. Give me a mandolin over a synthesizer any day."

Carmen dipped her spoon into the sundae that the waitress had placed between them and thought about this. She knew that Drew liked music he thought was raw and real. And she'd been hearing Kate play her guitar almost constantly the last few days, and from what she could tell, Kate was definitely sounding rawer. Realer.

Like maybe she didn't want to be Katy Perry after all. She'd even mentioned something about playing an open mic. And playing *well*, of all things. Not a second of stage fright.

"I sort of wonder if Kate might be rethinking her musical direction," Carmen said.

Drew raised an eyebrow. "What makes you say that?"

Carmen told him what she knew about Kate's open

mic, which wasn't much. Kate hadn't told her about it until it was over, after all. Carmen tried not to feel offended that Kate had managed to invite Madison, who was definitely not her idea of a supportive crowd, despite the peace she'd brokered between them.

"So she didn't panic? She kept her cool?" Drew sounded both surprised and happy.

"Apparently she was great," Carmen said. "Not a single slipup." She wished she could have seen it. She still respected and liked Kate a lot, despite the various problems they'd had, and she was glad they were on friendly terms again. She wanted to make sure they stayed that way. Kate might have her annoying moments, but she'd never willfully hurt anyone. Unlike Fawn.

"Good for her," Drew said. "That's awesome."

"You should help her out. Put in a good word with your bosses. They might really love Indie Kate," Carmen suggested.

Drew nodded thoughtfully. "Like, say, your dad?"

"Couldn't hurt. And you should also call her," Carmen said. "To talk."

"I will," Drew said. "Soon." His eyes searched her face. "I think she always thought there was something between you and me so the kiss really struck a chord," he said quietly.

Carmen laughed breezily to cover up the jolt she felt at those words. "There are quite a few years of friendship between us, Drew," she said. "We've got a lot of history."

She knew that wasn't what he was talking about, but she wasn't ready to let the conversation head in that direction. She was finally feeling like she was on her feet. The last thing she needed was something else to knock her off-balance.

"Right. Which was why I was so hurt when you didn't tell me about your pregnancy," he teased.

Carmen put her face in her hands. She couldn't believe she still had to hear about this. "That's over, you know," she said, looking up at him again. "I'm sure Kate told you, but I figured out that it was Fawn all along. And then Laurel talked to some people who knew her, and she found out that Fawn basically stalked me. She signed up for the acting class I was in specifically so she could meet me. She manipulated her way into being my friend. And when I didn't help her career as fast as she thought I should, she turned on me."

Drew nodded. "That's pretty crazy. Craving fame does weird things to people. I'm sure she was a decent girl once." He took an enormous bite of sundae, nodded approvingly, and then helped himself to another.

"You're much too generous and forgiving," Carmen said. "I know you never liked her very much, and I just want to say, I hereby give you veto power over all my potential friends and dates. Please use it."

"What about you and Luke?" Drew asked, his mouth still full of whipped cream.

"That's over, too," Carmen said. "He's dating his costar."

"Why am I not surprised about that either?"

"Because it's a Hollywood cliché," Carmen said. "Leading man falls for leading lady, sparks fly on set, they leave their wives/girlfriends/kind-of-girlfriends, and then they ride off into the proverbial sunset."

"As far as I'm concerned, Luke can take a long ride off a short pier," Drew said. "I never liked him much, anyway."

"I know, I know. Hence the veto power, all right? Now push over that sundae where I can reach it."

For a while they simply sat there, enjoying each other's company. There was no one in the world Carmen felt more comfortable with. How had she forgotten that? She'd gotten so wrapped up in the drama of the show and her friends (or "friends") that she'd practically written Drew out of her life. She made a vow that something like that would never happen again.

"Your phone's vibrating," Drew pointed out.

Carmen picked it up and read the text from Kate. OMG! SOPHIA IS ACCUSING TREVOR OF SEXUAL HARASSMENT. Her jaw dropped. "You have got to be kidding me," she said.

"What?" Drew asked.

When Carmen told him, Drew burst out laughing.

"Is that the appropriate response?" Carmen demanded.

"Yes," Drew said, still laughing. "I'm sorry, but it is. This world you're in is so insane that nothing surprises me anymore."

"But poor Trevor!" Carmen said.

"Poor Trevor nothing," Drew laughed. "Play with fire, and you're going to get burned. He's been taking advantage of that girl's crazy for a while now. I'm not surprised it came around to bite him in the ass."

Carmen shot him a look. "Don't like Trevor much, either, do you?" she asked, to which Drew shrugged non-committally. "Well, anyway, there's no way it's true. He cares way too much about the show to ever endanger it like that. Plus, I can't imagine him having actual feelings for another human being."

"Isn't he married, though?"

"Yes, but none of us have ever met her. Suspicious, don't you think?"

Drew shrugged again. "Well, it's definitely an inconvenience for the guy. Sophia's putting him in a bad position. But he'll come out on top."

Carmen took the cherry from the sundae dish and popped it into her mouth. She had to admit she agreed with that. Trevor *always* seemed to come out on top.

31

THE SOURCE OF SO MUCH DRAMA

"I'm telling you, Trevor came on to me," Sophie said. She was swirling her swizzle stick around in her drink, but she looked up at Madison with the full force of her lovely blue eyes, as if begging to be believed.

Madison quickly glanced away. "Okay. Why don't you tell me about it?" she said. She didn't buy Sophie's story for a moment, but she'd let her spin the lie a bit longer. It had been a dull, quiet morning, and Sophie's insanity was about to make it interesting, at least for a short while.

Sophie took a deep breath, then let it out, long and slow, as if she had to gather strength to begin. What, did she think she was on *Dr. Phil*? "We were in his office, and it was the afternoon, and he asked me if I wanted something to drink. I assumed he meant water, so I said yes. The next thing I knew he was handing me a glass of wine and sitting down next to me on the couch. And he said to me, 'You know, Sophia, I've always admired you. . . .'"

On second thought, it wasn't actually that interesting,

Madison realized. She didn't really care what fiction Sophie was going to come up with. Considering the amount of daytime television Sophie watched, Madison could probably guess the rest of the story. Her eyes darted to the April issue of *Vogue* on her coffee table. Could she thumb through that while still faking active listening?

Or maybe she could check her email. She was expecting a note from Jack Stanbro any day now. Madison had polished up her ideas and sent them off, and he'd called her excitedly. What followed was another very interesting conversation about Madison's future—perhaps as the reigning queen of Gallery's Wednesday night lineup. And it was always fun to see how many love notes she'd gotten @missmadparker. . . .

"Are you listening, Madison? He wants to fire me now because I wouldn't sleep with him."

"Wow, that really sucks," Madison said absently. "What are you going to do?"

"I told you what I'm doing. I've filed an official complaint and I'm talking to my lawyer about a civil suit."

"Maybe you should call Dad and have him kick Trevor's ass," Madison suggested. "Although Trevor *has* been working out a lot lately. . . ."

"You're not taking this seriously."

Madison finally met her sister's gaze. She wanted to say: *And tell me, please, why I should? For one thing, Trevor would never jeopardize his precious show like that. And for another, if he did, it wouldn't be for you, with your beaded necklaces and*

reject-from-1969 fashion. It would be for someone like . . . me.
But instead she said, "I'm sorry, do go on."

Sophie stared at her for another minute and then began talking. "It isn't right, taking advantage of his power like that. He knows I'm vulnerable. He knows he has me where he wants me. It's the very definition of sexual harassment."

Madison got up to rearrange the pillows on the couch. She was starting to feel disturbed. She'd thought that Sophie was laying down the lies pretty thick, but it was beginning to sound as if she actually believed them.

She remembered the personality tests Trevor had asked them to take. While she had chosen, instead, to sign a document indemnifying *The Fame Game* and all its producers, writers, etc., against any harm she felt she might have received, she suspected that Sophie had taken the test. What had it revealed? Madison wondered if she could get Trevor to tell her.

There was a tiny, troubling voice in the back of Madison's head, and it said: *Maybe Sophie would have turned out to be less insane if you'd stuck around, instead of hitting the road to Hollywood.*

But it wasn't Madison's job to take care of her sister, any more than she already had through the miserable years of her childhood. It was their *parents'* job, and if they couldn't do it—well, the blame fell on them. Not her.

Sophie was still talking. "What?" Madison asked, turning back around.

"You're my sister," Sophie said, "and you have to

support me." She crossed her arms across her chest. "You supported Dad, for God's sakes, and what did that guy ever do for you?"

These words almost physically *hurt* Madison. The fact was, Charlie had done nothing for her except screw up her life. (Although he'd been around for almost a week this time and so far he hadn't stolen a thing!) But Madison couldn't help it; she loved him. She knew he didn't mean to be such a disaster. He just wasn't very good at being an adult. He'd never had a good father—how was he supposed to know how to be one? Whereas Sophie . . . Sophie's betrayals seemed significantly more calculated.

"It's true, I supported Dad," Madison said. "And I've supported you by allowing you to be a part of my show."

"You're not the boss of it," Sophie grumbled, sounding suddenly like a five-year-old. "It was Trevor's call."

"Right, and now it's Trevor's call to fire you."

Sophie sat up straight. "Madison," she said pleadingly. "I need you. You have to help me out."

Madison nodded. "Fine. You're right. You're my sister. I'll make my statement tomorrow."

Madison decided to take her time calling Sasha, her publicist, the next day. She worked out for two hours, then met Kate and Gaby for a quick caffeine fix at Coffee Bean & Tea Leaf.

"You need a haircut already," Madison told Kate, lightly tugging at a straggly end. "How could that be?"

"I have something to confess," Kate said, tucking the piece behind her ear.

Madison shot her a sharp look.

"I'm letting my hair grow out again," Kate said. "It was fun while it lasted, but . . . I think it's a little too edgy for me."

"Suit yourself," Madison said. "Just please, please consult with me on the color, all right? Don't you dare box-dye it. And that strawberry-blond thing you had going was way too Midwestern. You looked like a camp counselor."

Kate laughed. "You are without a doubt the meanest person I've ever been friends with," she said.

"And you love me anyway," Madison said with a smile.

"You're right," Kate answered. "I do."

"I do, too," Gaby said. "Even though you banned my smoothies from the apartment and threw out the blouse my nana gave me."

Madison wrinkled her nose. "Because your smoothies smelled like *compost*. Just be a normal person and get them at Pressed Juicery like everyone else. And that blouse made you look homeschooled. It was an act of kindness to toss it."

"Does Pressed Juicery deliver?" Gaby wondered. Then she got distracted by the rack of magazines by the door.

Kate tapped Madison on the hand. "Are you going to make your statement soon?"

Madison nodded. "I wrote it last night." She turned her laptop around so that Kate could see the screen.

"'My sister, Sophia Parker, has been the source of so much drama both on screen and off,'" Kate read. She laughed. "*I'll* say. 'While I love her deeply and wish to support her as much as possible, I cannot stand by while she makes baseless accusations against our producer.' Wow, you sound totally professional. Did you ever consider law school?"

Madison scoffed. "I'm too pretty for law school. Keep reading."

"Clearly you haven't seen *Legally Blonde*," Gaby chimed in.

Kate bent down to the screen and read the rest. "'Trevor Lord is an innocent man, and everyone involved with *The Fame Game* knows it, including my sister. Her accusations are a cry for help. At this point, I offer my support in saying that I hope she gets that help, so that she can work through the issues that lead her to wreak such havoc on the lives of those around her.'" Kate sat back and ran her hands through her hair. "Wow," she said again. "Are you sure about this, Madison? This is going to devastate her."

Madison nodded grimly. "Believe it or not, I'm not happy about doing this. But she needs help, and what else is going to make her get it? She's certainly not going to listen to me."

"So how does it work?" Kate asked.

Madison gave one final glance at her letter and then pressed Send. "It goes to my publicist, who's giving it to Veronica Bliss at *Gossip* as an exclusive." She shrugged.

"And then it gets picked up by Just Jared, Perez, TMZ, and everyone else in the world. And my little sister realizes that her game is up."

Madison honestly didn't want to hurt Sophie; she hoped her statement would encourage her to seek treatment. But if Sophie didn't—if, say, she struck back and accused Madison of covering up her own (nonexistent) affair with Trevor—well, Madison had Dr. Garrison, psychiatrist to the stars, on speed dial.

She'd called him up after Kate's on-camera meltdown last season and suggested that he might want to be a little more *careful* about scribbling out prescriptions. She hadn't threatened him in any way, of course, but she had made him nervous. (She hadn't mentioned that it was actually Gaby's Xanax that caused the disaster, but what Dr. Garrison didn't know wouldn't hurt him.)

In other words, Madison had a backup plan. She really did hope that Sophie would try to get help. But if she didn't, Madison was sure that a couple of guys showing up at her door with a straitjacket would make for a really good episode of *The Fame Game*.

32

ANOTHER CHANCE

Drew was waiting for Kate outside the Rock It! offices. He had his hands in his pockets, and he was slowly pacing back and forth. Kate watched him for a moment before he saw her. She took in his shaggy dark hair, his familiar slouch, the edges of his tattoos peeking out from beneath his oxford.

Her heart fluttered in her chest. Was it from missing him, or for what she was about to do?

In less than an hour, she would be going in to play for executives at Rock It! Records. When Todd, her manager, told her the news, it sounded as if he couldn't believe it himself. "Rock It! Records," he'd practically squealed. "They've *never* called me before. But apparently they've been hearing great things about you, and they want a meeting."

Kate did a lot of jumping up and down and silent screaming (good thing she was alone in the apartment). Drew may have told her they needed to take a break, but he'd still come through for her; he'd obviously talked her up to the Rock It! people. Then she and Todd had set the date, and she'd agreed to bring in new songs. Now here she was. Staring her future, good or bad, in the face.

She headed up the walkway, Lucinda knocking against her leg. "Hey, Drew," she said, feeling shy.

He looked up at her and smiled. "Hey, yourself," he said.

She pointed to the bench next to a small fountain, which was in the shape of a treble clef. Water snaked down the sides, making a soothing sound that failed to soothe her.

They sat, almost touching but not quite. Instead of looking at each other, they watched the traffic go by on Santa Monica Boulevard.

Kate took a deep breath. "When I messed up my showcase, I thought I had ruined my chance at making it," she said. "But now I have another chance. So I really owe you."

"You don't owe me anything," Drew said.

"What do you mean? You obviously said something for them to consider me." She smiled ruefully. "Kate Hayes, the one-hit wonder."

Drew put his hands on his knees, and Kate was struck again by how long his fingers were. He could span an octave and a half on a piano keyboard, no problem. It occurred to her suddenly that she had never heard him play. How messed up was that? She'd been so set on her own music that she'd never asked to hear his. No wonder he'd gotten tired of her.

"Actually, I wasn't the one who convinced them," he said.

Kate looked at him in surprise. "Then how—"

"It was Carmen," he said.

"Carmen?" Kate repeated. The surprise had turned to shock.

"You guys are friends, right? Is it really that hard to believe?"

Kate was torn between an overwhelming feeling of gratitude to her roommate and confusion about Drew: Why hadn't he spoken up for her? Did he think she wasn't good enough?

"Well . . . ," Kate began, but then she stopped. She didn't know what to say. She'd never dreamed Carmen would step up in that way—not because Carmen wasn't a friend, or a good person, but because honestly, she didn't seem to care that much about music. Philip Curtis might as well have been a tax accountant for all the interest Carmen took in his work.

"I backed her up, though," Drew said. "In case you were wondering."

Kate nodded. "I was."

"I guess a few days ago, Carmen emailed her dad one of the songs you've been working on. Philip really likes to find new artists, but he doesn't get to that often anymore because he's always working the business side of things."

"So it's because I'm friends with Carmen?"

Drew laughed. "He's way too busy to take a meeting out of the kindness of his heart. He thought the song was great."

"Did he tell you that?" Kate asked.

"As a matter of fact, he did."

Kate sighed. She wasn't sure if she felt less pressure now, or more. "Wow."

Drew said, "You've got to feel confident when you go in there today. You've got to show them what you can do, all by yourself—no backup, no synth, no Auto-Tune."

"Are you going to be there?" She couldn't keep the hope from her voice.

Drew shook his head. "I'd like to be, Kate, I really would. But I have a class in thirty minutes."

Her heart sank. "Oh."

"But you don't need me. You think you do, but you're wrong. The song that Carmen sent to her dad? I hadn't even heard it before. You wrote it, sang it, and recorded it by yourself, and in my humble opinion, it's pretty damn great."

Kate told herself it was true. Somehow she'd turned a corner, and it wasn't thanks to a prescription or yoga or whatever that weird tapping therapy was called. It was because she'd remembered the joy music brought her. And, maybe even more importantly, the joy it had brought her dad.

There was a line from a poem he used to quote: "He

who hears music, feels his solitude peopled at once." It had always seemed a little stuffy to Kate, but lately it had seemed right. When she was fighting with Carmen, and then later with Drew, her music had kept her company. She had not been alone.

"I don't have to tell you how talented you are," Drew went on.

"I was selfish," she began. She wanted to tell him how sorry she was that she'd gotten swept up in her desire to be famous. She wanted him to know that she hoped to hear his music too.

But Drew cut her off. "It's not selfish to want to share a gift," he said. He leaned forward and clasped his hands together. "I wish I had half your talent."

"Oh, Drew, please," she said.

"Seriously. You don't have to study composition at UCLA because you can already write really good songs. What you have can't be taught. It's just a part of who you are." He turned to look at her. "That's why you're going to be great in there."

She smiled at him. "Do you want to hear the one I wrote for you?" she asked.

His eyes widened. "Um, yeah, okay."

He watched as she took out Lucinda. She was going to play outside, on the street, like a busker! Who knew, maybe someone would walk by and toss her a dollar.

"What's it called?" Drew asked.

"It's called 'Thank You,'" she said.

And then she sang the song about the girl and the boy who wanted to belong together but didn't. And how the girl would never forget the boy, not as long as she was still singing.

She sang it with tears in her eyes. And when she was finished, Drew pulled her into a long, hard hug.

"You're going to be amazing," he whispered into her hair.

"Thank you," she said. "*Really.*"

And then she waved good-bye to him and walked toward the double doors of Rock It! Records, knowing that her future was riding on the next hour. She hoped beyond hope that everything would be all right.

33

TOTALLY UNEXPECTED

"Hey there, miss, you need a ride?"

Madison smiled as she pulled open the door of Ryan's brand-new vintage Mercedes and slid gracefully into the passenger seat.

He grinned back. "Nice dress."

She plucked at the hem of the Alexander McQueen mini. "What, this old thing?" "This old thing" was a serious splurge; it had cost her a cool $1,300. (Which was enough for a down payment on a trailer in Armpit Falls—not that Madison was *ever* going back there again.) "Nice car," she added.

"I thought you might like it," Ryan said. "I bought it from a friend of my dad's. He gave me a deal, because he says I found him the perfect dog." Then he grinned. "You're not going to believe who it is."

Madison widened her eyes. "*Not* Tiny—"

Ryan nodded. "Tiny," he confirmed.

Madison laughed. "Well, good for Mr. Bitey. I guess

he shaped up once he got the taste of the high life."

"Beverly Hills is a lot cushier than Lost Paws, that's for sure." Ryan pulled into the street, then headed toward Venice. "Gjelina still okay with you?"

"Sounds great." Gjelina was his favorite Italian place. In other words, they were not going to an El Segundo hole-in-the-wall or some Topanga Canyon hideaway, the way they used to. Unless Ryan and Madison magically turned invisible, they were going to be seen. Together. In public.

Which was exactly what had caused all the problems between them last time. But if Ryan wasn't worried about it anymore, why should she be? Maybe he'd managed to shake his nearly pathological hatred of cameras.

(Madison had a moment of uncertainty then; should she alert her favorite paparazzo? Because if pictures of her and Ryan were going to appear—and surely they would—shouldn't they be as flattering as possible? Lorenzo always made her look so glamorous. . . . But then she slipped her phone back in her purse without dialing him. She was going to have to take her chances.)

"You want to put the top down?" Ryan asked.

Madison nodded enthusiastically. She didn't care if it ruined her new blowout. Today was the first truly warm day they'd had in weeks. Yesterday's rain seemed to have washed the sky clean, and now, in the late afternoon, it was a bright and endless blue.

Madison watched a mother herding two young daughters

across the street. The older one looked quietly furious, and the younger one was wailing. Madison felt a pang of recognition. "So Sophie's begun an outpatient treatment program," she said, watching the little one attempt to kick her sister in the shins.

"Good for her," Ryan said.

"Yeah, because a taste of the high life didn't straighten *her* out at all."

"Maybe this will."

"I'm not holding my breath," Madison said.

Of course she hoped Sophie got her head together. She had withdrawn her accusations of sexual harassment against Trevor, which was a step in the right direction. Madison suspected, though, that she'd done it for purely selfish reasons: Sophie realized that if she bit the hand that fed her, no other hand was going to show up. Ever. And while she might not have a chance to get back on *The Fame Game*, there were a hundred other reality TV shows that might welcome her onto their cast.

Like *Psycho Bitches*—was that a show? If not, it should be, and Sophie should star in it.

Ryan cursed under his breath; a giant SUV had just cut into his lane and then slammed on his brakes. "Nice driving, TRY TOFU."

Madison squinted. "Is that really what his license plate says?"

"Yep—do you need glasses or something?"

As a matter of fact, Madison did. But she didn't like the

way they looked on her, and she was incapable of sticking fingers in her eye to put in contacts.

"It's like a cosmic message from Sophie," she said. "'I'm doing fine now—try tofu!'"

"You're funny," Ryan said. "And you have a funny family."

"That is the world's *biggest* understatement," Madison replied.

She gazed out the window; now they were stopped in traffic. She could smell exhaust and the faintest hint of early-blooming magnolias. She was struck again by how much she loved L.A. As crazy as it was, and as hard as life there could be, it was home to her.

"How's your dad doing?" Ryan asked. "He called the other day, but I missed it."

"He claims to have taken up jogging, but I'm going to have to see it to be convinced."

Madison still couldn't believe how friendly Charlie and Ryan had become. Apparently, Charlie was teaching Ryan all about the inner workings of his new-old Mercedes. And maybe, just maybe, Ryan was teaching Charlie how to be a responsible, upstanding human being.

"He's coming over for dinner next week," Madison added. "If you want to join us."

"Sure," Ryan said. "I've got this book I told him I'd lend him."

Oh, Charlie doesn't read, Madison wanted to say. But then again, what did she know? She'd also once insisted he didn't steal, and look how wrong she'd been.

She'd had a long heart-to-heart with him after Ryan brought him over for their continental breakfast reunion. They had agreed to see each other once a week, at an established time. "Like prison visiting hours," Charlie had said brightly.

"Noooo," Madison had corrected, "like a regular lunch date. You're in Los Angeles, remember? Not the county pen."

It was almost funny, except that it wasn't. Charlie needed to learn how to act like an adult, for maybe the first time ever. And Madison believed he was capable of it. She just had to make sure that their relationship got rebuilt *slowly*. Carefully. She'd learned the classic lesson last season: Actions speak louder than words. So Madison wasn't going to assume Charlie had changed simply because he said so; she was going to make him prove it—over a period of months, if not years.

And she was going to keep him far, far away from any jewelry stores.

"Something I've been meaning to mention," Ryan said, bringing her back to the present. "Lost Paws won a really big grant recently, and we're going to be expanding."

"That's fantastic," Madison said. "Congratulations."

"The cool thing is, we now have the money to hire a general handyman/Guy Friday type. Do you think Charlie would be interested?"

On impulse, Madison grabbed Ryan's arm and happily

squeezed it. "Oh, that would be *perfect*," she said. "He would love it." Then she realized that her hand was on his bicep—a cheek kiss seemed to be okay, but was fervent grabbing a no-no?—and quickly withdrew it. She sat back in her seat and stared out the window, confused all over again. She didn't know what was going on between her and Ryan, but whatever it was, she didn't want to mess it up this time.

"Good," Ryan said. "I'll give him a call."

Had he even noticed the way she'd gripped his strong arm? Did he have any idea how much she wanted to touch him again?

No, probably not.

She fingered the small diamond studs that she'd bought with her first reality TV show paycheck, back when she was the Bad Girl on *L.A. Candy*. Then she met her own blue-eyed reflection in the car's side mirror. *You have come such a long way since then*, she thought.

"I have some news, too," she offered.

"Tell me," Ryan said, trying to peer around the SUV. "And make the story really long, because we're not moving again anytime soon. I hate the 10 freeway."

"I don't think I'm going to be in front of the cameras that much longer," Madison said.

Ryan's head snapped in her direction. "What?"

She smiled at his shocked face. "I mean, there are always going to be paparazzi. At least I hope. But I think I'm going to . . . change my focus."

"You're not quitting reality TV, are you?" Madison could hear the hope in his voice, and she tried not to hold it against him.

"Not exactly. I'm going to *produce* it," she said. Saying it made her feel giddy and thrilled, even though nothing was certain yet. "I started a production company, Beautyland, a long time ago. I stopped paying attention to it for a while, what with all those animal cages I had to clean and dealing with my nightmare of a boss," she said pointedly, narrowing her eyes at him. He shrugged, smiling. "But I've been ramping it back up, and I've met with some people at Gallery. They're interested in working with me."

"Wow," Ryan said. "That's awesome."

She nodded. It *was* awesome. At this point, *two* of her ideas had been marked for likely production. She'd sent Jack Stanbro a bottle of Champagne in thanks, and he'd simultaneously sent her one in congratulations; she had a feeling she was going to like working with him.

She wondered if Kate would be interested in talking to Jack about a show focused on people trying to make it in the music business. Like *American Idol* but without the whole karaoke feel. The judges would be the various A&R execs. . . . Maybe the performers would all live in a house together. It'd be like *The Real World* but without the total crazies. And everyone on the music show would have *talent*. It could be called *House of Rock*. . . .

"Penny for your thoughts," Ryan said.

"My thoughts are worth way more than that," Madison

teased. But then she told him about all of her ideas, and he offered some of his own, and before they knew it, the traffic had cleared and they were pulling up to the entrance of Gjelina.

Madison took a deep breath as they exited the car. She wasn't going to worry about whether or not this was a date, or whether or not she and Ryan had a future. She was simply going to enjoy her time with him. She'd planned out so much of her life. She could afford to let this piece of it unfold naturally.

"Madison Parker," cried a voice. "Over here! Give us a smile."

She bit her lip and turned to Ryan. "Um—there's a photographer. I'm sorry. They're never in Venice. Do you want to turn around and go somewhere else?" She wasn't sure he was really okay with being photographed—even if he said he was.

What Ryan did next was totally unexpected. There, on the sidewalk outside Gjelina, in front of strangers, diners, and paparazzi, he took her hand, pulled her closer, and kissed her.

His lips were warm and soft, and then she was kissing him back, while her heart thudded in her chest and butterflies zipped around in her stomach. She'd never felt this way about anyone—she understood that now more than ever.

She also understood that Trevor was going to kill her for dating someone who wouldn't film. But she didn't care.

Finally, after all these years, she understood what happiness felt like.

It felt like this.

Everything else would come in time. She didn't know *exactly* what she wanted next, but she didn't have to. She was Madison Parker, after all, and whatever it was, she knew she was going to get it.

EPILOGUE

MOMENTS IN THE SUN

Now *this* was a red carpet, Madison thought, as the door of her town car slowly opened, revealing a crush of people and press outside the Chinese Theater that exploded all around her. She reached up to take Ryan's outstretched hand, and she could hear the shouts of the crowd getting louder by the minute.

Ryan looked a little nervous, but he was movie-star handsome in his Ralph Lauren Black Label tux, his hair lighter from the two weeks they'd spent on the beach in Miami. (It was a celebratory vacation, thanks to the excellent news from Jack Stanbro at Gallery.)

"You ready for this?" Madison asked her boyfriend, smiling.

"Ready as I'll ever be," he said, smiling back bravely. Over the last six months, since their date at Gjelina had rekindled their romance, he'd seen his picture printed a *lot*. He still didn't love it, but he'd learned to take it in stride.

Up ahead were dozens of screaming girls holding out

posters for *The End of Love*, which was premiering tonight. Madison thought back to the red carpet where she'd first seen Carmen, before she knew they'd be working together on *The Fame Game*—and how a supposed Madison Parker fan had rudely snubbed her the instant Carmen Curtis appeared. Tonight, though, Madison didn't feel a single twinge of jealousy. Her own moment in the sun was coming soon, and right now she could afford to let Carmen enjoy hers. Of course, it would be the first of many. Carmen had recently wrapped another movie. She was only a supporting character in it, but it had an amazing cast and was sure to be a hit.

Speaking of Carmen, the actress was already near the theater entrance, looking chic and romantic (very Julia Capsen, her character in the movie) in a gold, strapless Valentino gown with a long train. *Variety* had written that she was even better than Gwyneth Paltrow in *Shakespeare in Love*—and since Gwynnie had taken home an Oscar, things were looking pretty good for the Topanga Canyon silver-spooner.

Beside Carmen was Luke Kelly, grinning his trademark Aussie smile and waving to the screaming fans like a princess on a parade float. He'd left his new girlfriend at home—or maybe he was between romances. Again. It was hard for Madison to imagine she'd ever thought of having her publicist set up a date with him. She squeezed Ryan's hand, and he squeezed it back.

There came another wave of loud cheering, and

Madison turned to see Gaby striding up the carpet, beaming. She was toned, not emaciated anymore, thanks to her hours of practice and performance on *Dancing with the Stars*.

Who could have imagined that being on *another* reality show would be the best thing for Gaby? She'd quit drinking again, this time for good, and she'd managed to beat her addiction to Botox. And, to top it all off, she'd actually *won* the dance competition. When the results came out, no one was prouder—or more surprised—than Madison. (But she had to admit, Gaby *did* do a kickass tango.)

Madison motioned for Gaby to join her and Ryan near the bank of photographers. Gaby was unescorted, but her new boyfriend (her dance instructor, Isaac) would be joining them later, along with Lily, who was just getting back from a shoot in Las Vegas. Jay had found his way home to Long Beach, and no one had heard from Fawn at all. Neither, as far as Madison could tell, was missed.

"You look great, Gab," Madison said, giving her roommate a hug.

"You too," Gaby said breathlessly. "You picked the Marchesa!"

Madison nodded. "And my *own* accessories," she said, fingering the layered gold necklaces at her throat. They lacked the diamonds that her past red-carpet necklaces had boasted, but they had been a gift from Ryan, so they were worth much more. Besides, while Charlie had been behaving himself perfectly since his return, there was no reason to tempt him with more diamonds.

The two of them posed for photos together for a minute, then turned back to each other.

"Have you seen Kate?" Gaby asked.

Madison shook her head. "She probably got mobbed by eleven-year-olds even before she got to the carpet." Kate's most recent single, "Thank You," had been a major hit, and Rock It! was releasing her first album in a matter of weeks. Everyone was expecting it to be a smash, a perfect mix of folk-pop sweetness and indie bite.

Drew Scott was a producer on it, not to mention the cowriter on a handful of the songs. Once Kate got over her interest in hyper-produced music, they'd become a good team. Romantically, though, things had never really worked out between the two of them. (Madison suspected it might have something to do with the not-so-secret torch he carried for Carmen.)

"It turned out we were better in the studio than the bedroom," Kate had confessed. "But hey, at this point in my career? I'll take a good producer over a good boyfriend any day."

An admirable sentiment, Madison thought. But seeing as how Kate had been spotted around town with a young and handsome oil heir lately, maybe she was having her cake and eating it too.

"Madison, over here. Turn this way!" cried a photographer, and Madison obligingly gave him her best angle. (Although, really, she didn't have a bad one.)

Yes, things were looking good for everyone on *The*

Fame Game. Well, *almost*. Sophie was on some unnamed island off the South American coast, filming a knockoff *I'm a Celebrity, Get Me Out of Here*. Her communication with Madison was sporadic, thanks to the whole living-in-a-mud-hut thing, but from what Madison could tell, Sophie was seriously regretting her involvement. What was it she'd said? Something about not having toilet paper and eating fire-roasted crickets . . . ?

Poor thing! If Sophie ever made it back, maybe Madison would offer her a job as a PA on one of her *two* new shows with Gallery.

Or maybe not.

The first show was reality TV—Madison's specialty, obviously—but the second was actually a scripted comedy . . . about reality TV. (Hey, you write what you know.) Madison had sketched out the pilot, Jack Stanbro had set her up with a team of writers, and lo and behold, she was an executive producer of the future hit, *Get Real*.

Madison wondered if Trevor Lord had had any inkling of the success his girls would enjoy back when he assembled his *TFG* cast. Or of his own rise up the ranks of PopTV. She smiled, thinking of him. She loved to give Trevor a hard time, but she'd always be grateful to him for helping her become the star she was destined to be.

"Well," Ryan said, "I've had about enough of this posing. What about you?"

Madison laughed. In the old days, she would have said no, there was *never* enough posing. But she was different now. She linked her arm through Ryan's and stood on her tiptoes to give him a kiss.

"Let's go inside," she said. "I want to get a good seat."

She gave one final wave to the fans and the cameras. They'd still be here when the movie was over. For Madison Parker, the cameras would *always* be there.

ACKNOWLEDGMENTS

A special thanks to all the amazing people who made this book possible . . .

Farrin Jacobs, for making it through yet another book with me.

Emily Chenoweth, who helped every step of the way, even when the book tour stopped in Portland, Oregon.

Max Stubblefield, Nicole Perez, Kristin Puttkamer, PJ Shapiro, Dave Del Sesto, Matthew Elblonk, Maggie Marr, Sasha Illingworth, and Howard Huang as well as the team at HarperCollins: Sandee Roston, Ali Lisnow, Christina Colangelo, Melinda Weigel, Sarah Landis, Catherine Wallace, Gwen Morton, Josh Weiss, Cara Petrus, Sarah Nichole Kaufman, and Stephanie Stein.

William Tell for his musical expertise.

And as always a big thank-you to my friends and family. I love you all dearly, and you mean the world to me.

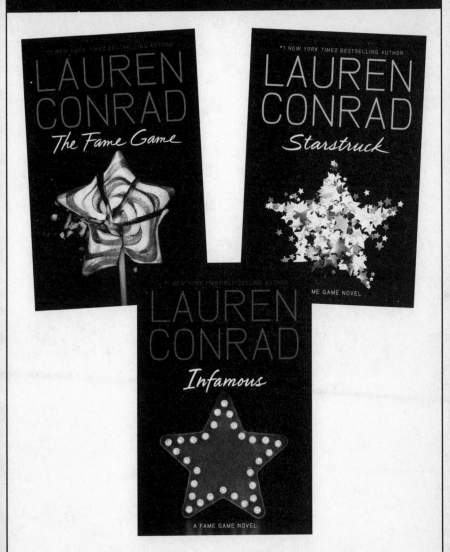